I0545002

A Woman Must Love

LAWRENCE BLOCK
writing as Sheldon Lord

A WOMAN MUST LOVE

LAWRENCE BLOCK writing as SHELDON LORD

Copyright © 1960 Lawrence Block

All Rights Reserved.

This is a work of fiction. Names, characters, places, and incidents are the products of the author's imagination or are used fictitiously. Any resemblance to actual events, locales, or persons is entirely co-incidental.

Cover and Interior Design by QA Productions

A LAWRENCE BLOCK PRODUCTION

CLASSIC EROTICA

21 Gay Street
Candy
Gigolo Johnny Wells
April North
Carla
A Strange Kind of Love
Campus Tramp
Community of Women
Born to be Bad
College for Sinners
Of Shame and Joy
A Woman Must Love
The Adulterers
The Twisted Ones
High School Sex Club
I Sell Love
69 Barrow Street
Four Lives at the Crossroads
Circle of Sinners
A Girl Called Honey
Sin Hellcat
So Willing

This is for
MARGE of Newport

CLASSIC EROTICA #12

A WOMAN MUST LOVE

Lawrence Block

CHAPTER 1

Her name was Barbara Sussex. She was a Buffalo girl all the way, born in Children's Hospital, brought up with two brothers and a sister in a white frame house on Norwalk just a mile or so from where she lived now. Eight years in grammar school at P.S. 66, four years at Bennett High School, four more years at the University of Buffalo. Her name then had been Barbara Mayo, but less than a year after she met Dana Sussex her name was changed from Mayo to Sussex by the relatively simple expedient of marriage.

Their marriage was probably inevitable from the day they met. She was in her senior year at UB; Dana was finishing his last year at UB law school and getting ready to take the bar exams and go into his father's practice. It was love at first sight, or close enough to pass for it, and after their first date neither of them ever dated anybody else. They kept discovering things that they had in common. Both of them liked the same books, listened to the same music, knew the same kind of people.

They met in early October and they were married before the end of June. After a brief ceremony with just the family present they drove to Niagara Falls for their honeymoon. They joked about it at the time and joked about it afterwards—Niagara Falls is just twenty-five miles from Buffalo and it's something of a busman's holiday for a Buffalo couple to spend a honeymoon there.

But the honeymoon was all either of them could ask for. The first night they made love for the first time and found out that the pleasure they gave to each other was the most wonderful thing in the world. During their courtship they both had gone half-crazy with desire for each other, but Barbara was a virgin and Dana was experienced enough and unselfish enough so that he was willing to wait until they were married.

It was worth waiting for.

The honeymoon never ended. For a year Barbara put her teaching degree to use and taught third grade at the same grammar school she had graduated from while Dana got going in his father's practice. Then one morning his father keeled over of a heart attack and Dana had to handle the whole business himself. It was a one-man office—Benjamin Sussex had never taken a partner. Now it was Dana's responsibility and it wasn't easy.

She quit her teaching job and went to help out at the office. She was a smart girl and before long she developed into the best secretary the office had ever had. And she discovered that she liked the work. It gave her a chance to be with Dana eight to ten more hours of the day than would have otherwise been possible—that alone made it worthwhile.

So everything was fine. The only problem was that they couldn't have any children, but that was something that neither of them minded too horribly. They already had their names on the waiting list at a reliable adoption agency and knew that whatever child they adopted would be as much theirs as one she carried in her womb for nine months.

Everything was fine.

Until the pain that Dana noticed in his chest one afternoon

turned out to be a tumor, which in turn turned out to be malignant.

Then the operation turned out to be a failure.

The double bed they shared turned out to be a deathbed. The man Barbara loved more than she loved life was turning, day by day and hour by hour, into a corpse.

"Babs."

He was calling her, she realized dimly. She shouted *I'm coming, honey* and grabbed a dishtowel from over the stove to dry her eyes. She didn't want him to see that she had been crying. It was hard enough for him as it was without adding to his worries.

She stopped in the downstairs bathroom and freshened up her face with cold water. Then she took a deep breath, thinking *I must look beautiful for Dana, I must be cheerful and bright and beautiful for him, I must be happy and sweet and alive and dry-eyed.*

She took the stairs two at a time and paused at the top for a second to catch her breath. *Everything's fine*, she told herself. Then she walked down the hall and into the bedroom.

He wasn't sitting up. For the past several days he hadn't been sitting up much at all and, while he never said anything about it, she could guess that he was getting weaker. But nothing showed in her face or in her voice when she smiled and said: "What is it, honey?"

"You didn't have to run. I just felt like seeing you."

"I didn't know you were awake."

"I've been up for about fifteen minutes. Tried to doze off again but I couldn't."

She sat down on the edge of the bed and took his hand between the two of hers. His fingers looked thinner every day, she noticed. She looked down at him, seeing how handsome he looked even with his skin so terribly pale and his cheeks sunken in. He'd been losing weight constantly until his ribs showed but he still looked good to her, still looked like the most handsome man in the world.

His hair was coal-black and wavy and he always kept it neatly combed. Even now when all he did was lie in bed all day his hair was combed carefully. His eyes were a deep brown and looked even darker than usual in the pale face. He was tall—well over six feet in stocking feet. Normally he was heavy although he didn't have an ounce of fat on him. But now . . .

"I missed you last night, Babs."

Up until a week ago she had slept with him, just as she had always done. But now the doctor had said that it would be better for her to let him have the bed to himself. She slept on the extra bed in a room across the hall—the room that would have been the nursery.

"I missed you," he said again, his voice gentle. "I just can't get used to waking up without you lying here next to me. Guess you've been spoiling me."

"I missed you, too."

"Did you?"

She nodded, not trusting herself to speak. She didn't think she'd be able to talk just then without showing how sick she felt inside.

"Babs?"

"What is it, honey?"

"Baby, why don't you climb out of those clothes and jump into bed?"

His eyes twinkled as he said the words and she felt herself blushing involuntarily. He had a way of keeping her off-balance even after all the years they had been married, and their sex life had remained spontaneous and exciting to both of them with the passing of years.

"Dana—"

"C'mon," he coaxed. "See how fast you can peel off those rags."

She took a breath and held it and worried lines appeared in her forehead. "Dana," she began, "do you think—"

"What's the matter?"

"I just thought . . . you know . . . it might not be good for you, Dana."

His face fell and for a long moment he didn't say anything. She felt as though it was her turn to speak now but she couldn't think of anything to say.

"Are you sure that's it, Babs?"

She looked blank.

"Or don't you want to sleep with me any more?"

"Dana!"

"I'm not blaming you," he went on bitterly. "I'm not much to look at any more, am I? I guess—"

Her head reeled and she pitched forward, her face buried in his chest. She let herself cry then for several seconds while he stroked her hair wordlessly. Then she got a grip on herself and sat up again, rubbing away tears with the heel of her hand.

"You know that's not it," she said. "I . . . I want you more than ever, now."

"I'm sorry," he said. "Forgive me, Babs. That was rotten of me."

"I just thought it would be bad for you. I thought, I mean . . ."

He took her hand and his eyes were deeper and sadder than she had ever seen them. His voice when he spoke was low and very determined and he spaced his words carefully.

He said: "Babs, I don't care if it's good or bad for me. I don't care if I drop dead two minutes after we're finished, can't you understand that? If I can't make love to my wife I might as well be dead."

"Don't talk like that!"

"Why not? It's true, Babs. I don't want to lie around waiting to die." He forced a smile. "C'mon," he said. "Get those goddamned clothes off."

She stood up without a word and began to undress. She was wearing a plain white blouse and a wool skirt. She unbuttoned the blouse and slipped it over her shoulders, underhanding it easily so that it landed on a chair near her dressing table. Then, her back to him, she opened the clasp of the skirt and unzipped it, stepping out of it and tossing it where she had tossed the blouse. She straightened up and her hands reached around her back for the clasp of the bra.

"Stop a minute, Babs. Turn around and let me have a look at you."

She turned to him, her arms dropping to her sides. His eyes took in the clear skin with a trace of summer tan, the breasts that filled the bra, the brief panties that were stretched snug against full hips.

"You're a beautiful woman, Babs."

She didn't say anything.

"Okay," he said. "Now get rid of the underwear."

She unclasped the bra and took it off, stepped out of the panties. She put them both on the chair with the rest of the clothing and returned to the side of the bed.

"Now crawl in under the covers."

She obeyed. When she was in bed with him she helped him off with his pajamas, seeing how thin he was now, how thin and weak and defenseless he was. Then he took her in his arms and she didn't see anything because her eyes were shut tight and her mouth pressed hungrily against his, her lips parted for the kiss. His lips were very gentle with hers, his tongue gentle and yet insistent as it slipped between her lips and caressed the inside of her mouth. She felt the first stirrings of desire and her arms tightened around his body.

He let one of his hands run the length of her big beautiful body, starting at her throat and passing over one breast where it lingered for a moment, cupping the warm sweetness of her. Then his hand passed over her flat stomach and below. He touched her then in the special place where no other man had ever touched her, no man but Dana, and his familiar fingers touched her and stroked her and caressed her, causing her breathing to quicken, causing her arms to tighten their grip around him.

"Dana—"

They made love with the combination of familiarity and excitement that can be found only in the lovemaking of two persons who have been lovers for years and who yet never fail to find a new delight in each other's embraces.

The rain outside pounded against the bedroom windows; the wind howled in the trees and whipped against the side of the house.

She hardly heard the rain, hardly was aware of the wind. The world was standing still for her now, the whole world fixed and immobile for her.

Higher.

She was conscious now only of her body, only of her own body and Dana's body. All her flesh seemed alive now with a brand new life.

Faster.

The world was no longer standing still. Now it was spinning dizzily on its axis and she was caught up in the spinning of it, caught up and whirled higher and higher to a blinding peak of ecstasy.

They reached the peak together.

Then peace—deep and infinite peace, with Dana soft and weak and sobbing in her arms, with her hands stroking his back and holding him close to her, with the wind lashing the outside of the house like an insatiable taskmaster, with the rain coming down as though it would never stop, as though the rest of eternity would be spent with Dana in her arms and the wind howling and the rain pouring down.

After it was over he was very tired and ready to sleep again. She waited until he was sound asleep and then slipped noiselessly from the bed, showering quickly in the bathroom, then returning to her room and dressing once again. She left the room, leaving the door ajar so that she could hear him if he called her.

Downstairs again she collapsed into an armchair in the living room and lit a cigarette. The first two tries her hand was shaking so badly that the match went out before she could get the cigarette burning, but on the third try she made it and sank gratefully into the chair with the cigarette between the second and third fingers of her left hand and the smoke deep in her lungs. She let the smoke out slowly, watching it with infinite patience as it drifted to the ceiling in a heavy grey cloud.

He couldn't die, she told herself. That was all there was to it—he would have to get well, to get up from the bed and be better again.

She couldn't live without him.

Silently she berated herself for making love with him just a short while ago. It was wrong—it would weaken him and make the inevitable outcome of the disease just that much quicker in coming.

She shook her head suddenly, changing her mind. Dana was right—it was better to love him completely for a day than to pass up his love for a week. Those moments of love had been worth quite a bit to both of them—a good deal more than the day or week of nothingness that might or might not have been their price.

She took another drag on the cigarette; this time the smoke tasted foul in her lungs and she butted the cigarette angrily in an ashtray on the table next to her. *I've got to be calm*, she told herself. *I've got to learn to live with this for as long as it lasts. I owe him that much. I can't be dragging my tail in the mud and crying all the time. He's got enough problems as it is.*

She hauled herself out of the chair and went to work cleaning the house, vacuuming rugs, washing her breakfast dishes and the dishes left over from last night's dinner. She made fresh coffee and had a cup for herself when it was ready, the coffee good and hot and rich.

The coffee, plus another cigarette, helped a little. So did the housework—it gave her a chance to forget to think about herself for a few minutes, and she was grateful for the chance.

She made lunch for Dana—a bowl of chicken broth, three slices of cinnamon toast, a cup of coffee. She started to boil water for tea at first but then she changed her mind and poured him a cup of coffee instead. Tea was for sick people; it would be better to give him coffee.

When she walked into the bedroom again he was propped up on the two pillows and his eyes were open. He smiled at her and she smiled back and set the tray down on the table next to his bed.

"Hungry?"

He nodded, then wrinkled his face when he saw what was on the tray. "Toast and soup," he said. "Regular hospital breakfast."

It was what the doctor had suggested, but she was very glad that she had settled on coffee instead of tea.

She helped him sit up and propped the tray on his lap. He began to eat and she wondered how long he would be able to eat by himself, how long before she would have to spoon the soup into his mouth for him. Then she forced herself not to think about it.

"Babs—"

She looked at him.

"That was good before, wasn't it?"

"It was wonderful."

"We're good together," he said. "Damned good. It's a shame we won't be able to do it much more but—"

He broke off when he saw she was at the point of tears again. He spooned more of the broth into his mouth and waited a minute before talking.

"You're a wonderful woman, Babs."

She didn't say anything.

"I don't want you to miss out on . . , well, on what we've had together. I'm going to die, Babs, but that doesn't mean that it has to be the end of the world for you as well. I don't want that to happen."

"What do you mean?"

He smiled gently. "I mean I want you to go on living. You're a young woman, honey—too young to be a widow forever. I want you to stay alive."

"I—"

"I don't know," he said. "Maybe it's not good form to talk about this, but sooner or later you're going to meet another guy, honey. And—"

She shook her head from side to side, unable to speak for the moment.

"Yes," he said. "You are, Babs. And I want you to. I know I'm going to die, but that's no reason for you to die too. You'll meet a guy and marry him and—"

He broke off and she couldn't say anything. They let the subject drop right there—he went on eating and she found something else to talk about.

Afterwards, washing the dishes, she thought about what he had said. It was just like Dana to be concerned about something like that, just like him to tell her she had his permission to remarry when the thought of being with anybody but him was enough to make her blood curdle.

She would never marry again, she thought. She had married once and she had gotten the best man in the world. That was enough. She would find something to do, something to keep herself busy. Maybe go back to teaching school—that might be the best thing to do. Dana had a large insurance policy plus some money saved, so she wouldn't have any financial worries, but she would have to do something to keep from losing her mind after he was gone.

She didn't want to think about it and she kept fooling herself, telling herself over and over again that the doctors were all crazy, that he wouldn't die, that any day now he would get up from his bed and be all right again and the two of them would be happy together for the next forty or fifty years. But telling herself this didn't do any good. She knew that it was just something she had invented to keep herself going, that Dana would die in a very short amount of time and that she would be left alone.

She thought back to their lovemaking. It had been so good, so perfect, and yet she couldn't help feeling that there was an odd note of finality about it, as if it was the end of something.

It was.

They never made love again. Three days later Dana was in a coma; a week later he was dead.

It rained the day he died and the wind howled in the trees all night long.

She followed his request and had the body cremated. Also in line with his request she took the ashes from the cremation and scattered them to the winds. It didn't seem fair to her that she was to have nothing of him for herself but that was the way he had wanted it.

"I couldn't stand rotting," he told her. "Lying in a grave forever. And there's enough valuable land being wasted on graves as it is without me adding to it."

The thought of winding up as ashes in an urn was equally unattractive. He wanted to go back to the earth, to be scattered in the wind. It was his right, of course, and she could see how he felt—but she couldn't help wishing that there were a grave or something, some special spot where she could go when she wanted to feel especially close to him.

She went back home. He was gone—dead, reduced to ashes and scattered to the wind. The house was empty in a way that it had never been before and she wondered how she was going to stand it, living in that house without him living there with her.

She would manage somehow, she thought. Dana wanted her to go on living and she would. Somehow, some way, she would make the best of her life. Her life without Dana.

But, she swore solemnly, no man would ever take his place.

CHAPTER 2

For two months she did nothing, nothing at all. Dana's affairs were easily settled—the insurance policy was paid and invested in a mutual fund that paid her a nice income, the law practice sold for a trifle of its value to one of Dana's associates. And with that taken care of Barbara quietly crawled into a neat little niche and lived in it. She left the house only to shop; the rest of the time she spent staring blindly at the television set or lost in a book or listening to a record on the hi-fi.

Friends—hers and Dana's—came to visit her, to try to cheer her up. She was always polite with them, always offered them drinks or coffee and sandwiches, always listened attentively as they spoke. But they could sense that she didn't care in the least whether they came to see her or not and in time they stopped coming. The denser ones took the hint when she turned down their invitations.

She gave up the world, gave it up completely. And, in the course of time, the world began to give up on her.

The rain continued well into the middle of November. Then it was replaced by a useless sort of snow that stayed white just long enough to reach the lawns and the sidewalks. There it turned at once to a grey and unpleasant slush.

Things kept happening in the outside world while she either

was unaware of them or let them come and go without caring enough to think about them. One team beat another team in the World Series. A dictator was assassinated in Latin America. The Carolina coast was slashed to ribbons by the worst hurricane in years. Forty-seven passengers and crew members were blown to hell when an airliner exploded seconds after takeoff at Dallas airport. A New York mother smothered her baby with a pillow when he cried in the middle of the night, then realized what she had done and slashed her wrists with her husband's straight razor.

Seven movie stars got divorces. A lunatic segregationist in Biloxi dynamited four churches and a synagogue in an effort to keep Negroes from going to school with whites. A family in central Ohio had their house sold for taxes rather than contribute to military spending.

A member of a juvenile gang in New York was castrated by members of another gang as reprisal for winking at the wrong girl. Three federal narcotics inspectors were jailed for looking the other way while heroin was distributed by a Chicago syndicate. *I Was A Teenage Paranoid* played to capacity crowds on 42nd Street; an excellent production of Garcia Lorca's *Blood Wedding* folded at an off-Broadway theater after three performances.

In short, human existence continued to move toward inevitable perfection during those two months. God was in his heaven and all was right with the world.

All was not right with Barbara Sussex. Nothing was right, as a matter of fact, and by the beginning of December she was beginning to realize this, beginning to see for certain that she couldn't go on the way she was going, couldn't continue to live alone by herself, to stay in the house on Covington Road twenty-four hours a day waiting for the world to end.

She had to do something. But there didn't seem to be anything to do, any course to follow. Day after day she told herself that tomorrow would be the proper day to get a job; tomorrow after tomorrow she decided that it would be a good idea to wait just one more day, to let just one more twenty-four hour period pass out of her life before doing anything. And the days went by.

Then, in early December, she decided that she couldn't take it another day. She would teach—her teaching degree was as valid as it had ever been, and almost every day editorials in the newspapers screamed about the crying need for teachers in the Western New York area. She considered calling the offices of the Board of Education but changed her mind. Instead she decided to take up where she had left off and dialed the number of the principal's office at School 66. The principal, Lester Antrim, was an old friend—her seventh grade teacher when she had attended the school years ago, her boss when she had taught there. He answered the phone and she told him who she was and what she wanted.

"Barbara!" he said. "Good to hear from you, my dear. I half-expected a call from you ever since I heard the terrible news about your husband. I can't tell you how sorry I am, Barbara."

She managed to pass that over.

"You could call the main office and get a steady job tomorrow," he told her. "The whole system's so overloaded it's positively terrifying. Do you know that we've got forty pupils in one fifth-grade class?"

She said something about how terrible it was.

"What can we do? If they won't give us the money for better education we simply won't have better education. But I'm getting off the subject, Barbara. What I started to say was that you could get a job at will, so to speak, but you might not wind up with quite what you're looking for. The Board of Education is mildly notorious for sending teachers who live in North Buffalo to jobs in South Buffalo so that the poor things spend two hours getting there in the morning and another two hours getting home at night."

He cleared his throat. "But," he went on, "if you're not in any particular rush I believe I have just the sort of thing you're looking for. Do you remember Miss Mary Monaghan? Taught seventh and eighth grade English?"

She said that she did.

"The poor thing had an accident," Antrim said. "Right in her own apartment she had a nasty fall and fractured her hip. You know what something like that means when you're her age. She'll be out at least through June and I think it's safe to assume she's thinking of permanent retirement. I've a temporary substitute here now but she's not at all qualified and she's due to leave at the end of next week if I can get hold of a replacement for her.

"Now if you're interested, Barbara, I can take care of everything for you. I'll clear it with the Board and you'll be assigned directly to 66 without going through all the official red tape."

She assured him that she was more than interested, that it was just what she wanted and much better than she had expected and that he should go right ahead and clear it for her. He told her to report for work a week from Monday unless she heard otherwise.

She waited until he hung up the phone, then replaced the receiver on the hook and went to the living room. She sat down in a chair to smoke a cigarette, thinking over the conversation with Lester Antrim, thinking that it would be good to get back to work again. Automatically her mind began reviewing the syllabus for seventh and eighth grade English, thinking of ways to make the material more exciting for her pupils, planning as much of what she would do in the classroom as she could without having a new look at the syllabus and without knowing anything about her students.

It was good, having something to do again, having another life outside of the walls of the house on Covington Road. Her mind and body already felt more nearly alive than they had since the day Dana died. She let herself relax completely in the armchair, running the fingers of her left hand through her corn-colored hair and trying to remember everything she had ever known about verbs and adverbs and dangling participles.

The job was even better than she had expected it would be. Just the experience of getting up at 7:30 Monday morning for a quick breakfast and then walking the five short blocks over Covington and down Parkside to the school was refreshing after so much time spent cooped up at home. She met Lester Antrim in his office before it was time for school to start and got the files and records on each of the thirty-one pupils in her home room plus fairly full particulars on her English students.

Teaching turned out to be a pleasure. While she didn't get

much English taught during the first few days, she found genuine delight in getting to know the children. They were a fine bunch—only one or two actual problem children, and even they were more mischievous than they were obnoxious. It was fun.

She got the seventh graders working on compositions while the eighth grade started in on *Huckleberry Finn*. By the end of the second week, with Christmas vacation starting, she had managed to wake her classes up, actually getting a few of them keenly interested in the material at hand.

But teaching was only a part of the excitement. Coming into contact with children was dramatic enough; coming into contact with adults again, and with two in particular, was even more dramatic.

Most of the teachers she already knew—the turnover was slow at a school like 66 and many of them had been around while she taught before—some had even had her as a pupil. There were several unfamiliar faces, however, and she got to know two of them right from the start.

She met Margo Kent in the teacher's lunchroom during lunch hour that first Monday. Margo looked as unlike the popular stereotype of a grammar school teacher as Barbara herself did. She was a small, black-haired woman with sparkling dark eyes—a woman, Barbara noticed, who managed to look sexy in glasses and a severely tailored charcoal suit. Her hair was curled in a bun on the back of her head and her mouth was smiling pleasantly when she introduced herself.

She was a very small woman. Everything about her was small from her delicate wrists to her equally delicate ankles. Her size and proportions coupled with an extremely pale complexion gave off an impression of daintiness, as if any physically or emotionally disturbing experience would knock her into Cattaraugus County.

Margo's personality cancelled out the impression neatly. She was warm and friendly and her conversation sparkled as brightly as her eyes. Almost before she knew it Barbara found herself talking animatedly to another human being for the first time in months. A moment later she had accepted a dinner invitation without realizing it, an invitation to have supper with Margo that very night.

Their friendship developed with a speed that astounded Barbara. Margo could keep a conversation going when Barbara had nothing to say and could listen sympathetically when Barbara felt like letting go of all the turmoil that had been building up inside her. The two of them hit it off perfectly and all at once Barbara was not so completely alone any more, not so much apart from the rest of the world. She had someone to talk with, someone to spend an occasional evening with, someone who cared if she lived or died. It made a tremendous difference.

Margo was one of the two teachers she met who made a strong impression upon her. The other was a man. His name was Curtis Tyrone.

Curtis Tyrone was either a man with two first names or a man with two last names, depending upon how you preferred to look at it. Whatever way you looked at it he was a man who didn't seem to fit. Not only didn't he match his job, but the various component parts of Curtis Tyrone didn't go well together.

He was a huge man with massive shoulders and a big barrel of a chest and flaming red hair that stood straight up on his head. Looking at him you would guess that he would have a big booming voice to match the shoulders and chest, but his voice when he spoke was always soft and quiet and well-modulated and his words were invariably chosen carefully and well. The voice and manner of speaking did not, at first glance, seem at all compatible with Curtis Tyrone.

Neither did his job. He might have fit into the academic world as a football coach. But he was not a football coach.

He was a guidance counsellor.

"Someone finally figured out that an assistant principal at a grammar school was about as essential as a fourth wheel on a tricycle," he told her once, explaining his job to her. "So they eliminated the position, which was good for the school system while it wasn't so good for all the assistant principals. They had things their way—all an assistant principal ever did was walk around counting the rolls of toilet paper in the stockroom."

He had grinned at her then. "But they couldn't give up the money. If they eliminated the position they would have had to let the city council cut the money set aside to pay assistant principals from the education budget. Some genius figured out that since it was impossible enough to get money into the budget there was no particular point in letting it get back out again.

"So," he went on, the grin widening, "they came up with the guidance counsellor. The guidance counsellor is an invaluable sort of fellow who takes the roughnecks and sits down to talk things out with them. Besides, *somebody* has to count the rolls of toilet paper in the stockroom."

She learned, though, that he was making his job sound a good deal less important than it actually was. Other teachers spent plenty of time talking about the way a boy or girl had miraculously ceased to cause trouble after a series of talks with Tyrone. And it wasn't just the troublemakers who learned to straighten up and fly right. There was a gawky little girl in the fifth grade who did marvelously on the IQ tests and managed to do so poorly in the classroom that her teacher wanted to leave her back a grade. After a few talks with Curt Tyrone the emotional problem that was holding the girl up was gently eased out of the picture and she began keeping up with her classmates.

There was a boy who sat on the sick bench every gym period, occasionally bringing a note from his mother asking that he be excused on account of some imaginary cold. Tyrone talked to him, got him to overcome his feelings of inferiority and develop a genuine interest in athletics. The kid would never play in the World Series—but he wouldn't spend any more gym periods on the bench.

There were more, many more. Most important of all were the children that the guidance counsellor recognized to need professional help. When it was necessary he recommended psychiatric therapy, therapy which might avoid more serious psychological problems in later life.

Barbara heard a lot about Curtis Tyrone and all that she heard was good. Everybody seemed filled with admiration for the husky redhead with the gentle voice.

It was easy to understand why. In addition to the great work he was doing, the man was possessed of an especially pleasing personality. He made good conversation across a table in the

lunchroom, good company when you were sharing a quick cigarette in the teachers' room between classes.

Barbara liked him.

And that's where the trouble started.

Because he liked her, too. He liked her very much and he
didn't try to keep the fact a secret.

And that meant trouble.

CHAPTER 3

"Mrs. Sussex?"

She turned at the sound of the voice. Curtis Tyrone was smiling down at her.

"There's a concert at Kleinhans Music Hall tomorrow night," he was saying. "They're doing a Mahler symphony and the Beethoven violin concerto. I was wondering if you might like to come with me."

She almost said yes without thinking. Then she shook her head more violently than she had intended.

"I thought we could have dinner first," he went on as if he hadn't noticed her shaking her head. "A quiet dinner and a pair of seats at a concert—pretty much the sort of way we teachers are supposed to spend an evening, wouldn't you say?"

She found herself smiling along with him. Then she cut off the smile just as she knew she had to cut off the invitation. "I'm awfully sorry," she said. "I'm afraid I'll be busy tomorrow night."

He didn't push. A shadow of disappointment passed over his face; then he grinned. "Should have asked sooner," he said. "Maybe I'll have better luck next time."

She was worried. Every day Curt Tyrone was beginning to represent more and more of a threat to the sort of life she wanted to lead. He seemed determined to date her, determined to get involved with her in one way or another.

And involvement with a man was something she did not want at all.

Dana was dead. That was fundamental. Dana was dead and she was his widow. He was the man she loved, the only man she had ever loved and the only man she would ever permit herself to love.

That was basic.

So what good would any dates with a man like Curtis Tyrone do for a woman like her? He was thirty-five and had never been married. He was a big, hearty, virile-looking man. He liked people and loved children. It didn't take a genius to figure out that he would want more from a woman than conversation across a dinner table and companionship at an occasional concert or movie.

Just what he might want was not entirely clear to her. The obvious answer was that he wanted what every man wanted, every man who wasn't impotent or homosexual and who hadn't lost an essential part of his anatomy in the war. The perfectly obvious answer, in short, was that Curtis Tyrone wanted to get into her pants.

For a moment she let her guard down and permitted herself to imagine what it would be like with him. She closed her eyes and pictured him beside her in bed, his big hands on her breasts and thighs, his mouth upon hers, his huge body above her, crouching over her. He would be whispering to her, whispering soft and gentle lovelies, and then the two of them would come together with the full passion of two animals in heat, moving together and—

No. She shook her head violently again, telling herself: *I can't even think this way. I can't think about such things, can't be disloyal to Dana even in my mind. I'm not a schoolgirl. I'm a widow who loved her husband and it isn't right to start having adolescent fantasies and sexy frustrated-virgin daydreams.*

But she couldn't help it. She couldn't help lying in bed at night and tossing and turning sleeplessly because she was all alone in the bed, all alone by herself with no one to make love to her. She couldn't help remembering the times she and Dana had made love again and again and again in that very same double bed, passing the whole night away like that, tasting the joy of each other's body over and over and over, passing up sleep for love.

She couldn't help wondering how she was going to go on, a red-blooded woman leading a dried-up life, a woman in the prime of life doomed to a life devoid of love. It didn't seem possible at times that she could go on like this, sleeping every night alone, tossing on her pillow like a damned soul squirming in hell.

Then, when she did sleep, then the dreams would come. The dreams were outright sex dreams, not symbolic things that only an analyst could unravel. The dreams were vivid and real to her, vivid and real and indescribably sensual.

One time she almost reached orgasm in her sleep—the dream was that real. Another time she woke up suddenly to discover that, sleeping, she had been trying to satisfy the dull ache in her groin with her own two hands.

Stop it, she would tell herself. *You've been a widow for less than three months. What's wrong with you—are you a cheap little tramp who only lives for sex? Can't you adjust to the state you're in?*

What the hell's wrong with you?

Curt Tyrone asked her out a second time, and when he did she found herself calling him Curt after he had called her Barbara instead of Mrs. Sussex. She regretted the familiarity as soon as it left her lips—it was natural at an informal school like 66 but it only made it that more difficult to turn down the second invitation as she had turned down the first.

The third time was harder. Christmas vacation had come and gone; the school year was half over. Curt caught up with her in the hallway on her way out the door that Tuesday afternoon and she had to stop and talk to him.

"Busy?"

"I'm on my way home," she said.

"Can I give you a ride?"

"I like to walk," she said honestly. "I can use the exercise."

"Even with all the snow on the ground?"

"It doesn't bother me. I've gotten pretty much used to it."

He produced a pack of cigarettes from his overcoat pocket and offered her one. She took one and put it between her lips; he lit hers and one for himself with a silver cigarette lighter. While he inhaled a mouthful of smoke she stood awkwardly, wanting to turn and go but forced to wait for him to speak.

"Mind if I walk along with you?"

She was speechless.

"I might as well get some exercise myself," he tried to explain. "Guess it can't hurt."

She was being subtly outmaneuvered and she found she didn't much like it. But what could she say? She nodded to him and they walked out the door and on through the playground to Parkside. He didn't try to take her arm and she was grateful to him for that much at least.

They walked a block while she waited for him to say something but he didn't say a word, walking in silence and smoking, then chucking his cigarette into a snow bank when he had finished with it.

Finally she said, "Why?"

"Why what?"

"Why did you want to walk with me?"

"Because I wanted to ask you out for dinner," he answered easily. "And then I want to find out what's the matter after you tell me you're busy."

"I—"

"Because you will tell me you're busy again."

She didn't say anything.

"Won't you?"

"Yes," she said with difficulty. "Yes, I suppose I will."

"Fine," he said. "See—I didn't even have to extend the invitation to get rejected. Now I'll ask why."

She hesitated. "It's . . . nothing personal, Curt."

"Want to talk about it?"

"It's not you—it's me. You know that my husband died just a few months ago. I loved him very much, Curt. He was quite a wonderful man."

He waited.

"I don't want . . . to see any other men. That's all there is to it, really. I don't want to date anybody or go out for dinner with anybody or . . . or anything."

"For how long?"

She didn't understand.

"For how long, Barbara? Are you going to refuse dates for the rest of your life?"

She thought about that one for a minute. "Yes," she said finally. "Yes, I guess I am."

"Look at me, Barbara."

It was a command and she couldn't help obeying it. Automatically she turned to face him.

"Is that the way your husband would have wanted it?"

She remembered what Dana had told her. "I don't think so," she said. "He wasn't a selfish sort of man. He even told me to feel free to remarry."

"And as a result you won't even go out to an innocent movie with a man?"

She shook her head, half-angry with him and half-angry with herself. "You don't understand," she said. "It's not just what he would have wanted—it's also what I want. I don't want to get involved with anybody, Curt. Definitely not now and probably not ever."

"Involved?"

She was silent.

"I'm not really asking you to get *involved* with me, Barbara. I'm trying neither to slip a ring onto your finger or to get my hands under your dress. All I'm asking—"

"The answer is still no."

His face fell.

"There are other women," she said, simply trying to find something to say. "I'm sure you could find somebody to keep you company, somebody who—"

"Don't make matches for me," he said a little roughly. "I'm a big boy now. I can take care of myself."

"I was only trying to—"

"I'm going to ask you out again," he told her. "Maybe after awhile you'll get bored with sitting in your house and staring at the walls. I'll see you tomorrow."

He turned and stalked off, headed back to the school where his car was parked. She watched him for a moment, then walked on home.

Tomorrow, she thought, she would drive her own car. That would eliminate any situations like the one she had just gone through. Much as she liked walking to work, much as she hated driving the convertible on a cold day, it was better than having to go through the gentle agony of a walk-and-talk with Curt.

She was beginning to see why he was so effective in his job. He knew just what question to ask, just when to wait her out. He could peel a person open and look inside without even working hard at it. It was frightening.

Another aspect of it all was even more frightening. It didn't look as though Curt Tyrone was solely interested in getting in her pants, as she had assumed. For one thing, if sex was all he was after he wouldn't be wasting so much time on her, not when she was such an unlikely prospect. Besides, his approach was the furthest thing in the world from a let's-turn-out-the-lights-and-go-to-bed pitch.

It was worse, she thought. His line was much closer to the let's-fall-in-love-why-shouldn't-we-fall-in-love approach, and if there was one thing she didn't want it was a man falling in love with her.

•   •   •

She told Margo all about it that evening. They were in Margo's apartment on Delaware Avenue, listening to a Schubert string quartet on the hi-fi and drinking black coffee.

"And so," she concluded, "he absolutely can't figure out why I don't go out with him."

"That makes two of us."

"Huh?"

"Let me put it this way," Margo said. "Why in the world don't you go out with him?"

"I already told you."

"You told me a lot of nonsense about not wanting to get involved."

"It's not nonsense!"

"The hell it's not. If it doesn't make any sense I call it nonsense. And if the crap you served up about not wanting to get involved makes any sense I'll eat it."

"Margo—"

"To begin with, Curt Tyrone is not attempting to get involved with you. That's point number one. Point number two is that even if he is, so what?"

"What are you talking about?"

"What I'm talking about ought to be perfectly obvious. What I'm trying to get across is that you're going to go stark raving mad if you don't find a man."

She was startled and it showed in her face.

"You were married once," Margo said. "Didn't you and Dana ever do anything in bed?"

She felt herself blushing.

"Don't turn colors, for God's sake. I'm a friend of yours—you don't have to play maiden schoolteacher with me."

She didn't say anything.

"For Christ's sake! Look, Barbie—if you keep on trying to lead the good life of academic widowhood you'll be climbing the walls within the year and beating your head against the side of a padded cell not long after. Is that what you want?"

"Margo—"

"Let me finish what I'm trying to say. Suppose, just for the sake of supposing because I strongly doubt it, but just suppose that all this redheaded Greek god is interested in is your lily-white body. Is that so horrible? He's probably fairly good in bed, for one thing, and in your position you can't afford to be too choosy."

It didn't seem possible that a sweet little schoolteacher like Margo Kent was saying these things.

"You're a woman," Margo went on. "Not a robot like most of the unmarried dolls at 66. To top it off you've been married and you presumably know what it's all about, although I admit you hide it well enough. How do you think you're going to go on living without a sex life?"

She couldn't resist it. "You seem to manage well enough."

Margo just stared for a moment. Then she threw back her head and burst out laughing. Her laughter was very loud for such a small woman.

"Oh, my God! Do you mean to say—"

And she started laughing again.

"My God, Barbie," she managed finally, "did you actually think—"

More laughter.

"Barbie, remember the times you've called me up and I told you I was busy?"

She nodded.

"Well," Margo said, "I was busy. And do you remember the times when you called me and I wasn't home?"

She nodded again, mystified.

"Well," Margo said, "I wasn't home. Now what in God's name do you think I was doing those times?"

She shrugged.

"You don't know?"

She shook her head.

"I was doing something which I hope I'll never get tired of doing," Margo said. "I was doing something which is about as important to me as eating or drinking or breathing.

"I was," she finished triumphantly, "sleeping with a man."

"Are you shocked, Barbie?"

She shook her head. "Not really," she said. "I'll admit I'm surprised, but *shocked* isn't the word for it. How come you've never—"

"Married? Honey, there's a world of difference between sleeping with a guy and living with him. The first is a ball but the second is my idea of nothing to do. I *like* the life of a maiden schoolteacher, all things considered. All but the maiden part of it, and I take care of that on my own. This is the twentieth century, honey. You may find this hard to believe, but there are quite a few gals at loose in the world who are loose in the world."

"I know that."

"Well, that's a start. Look, doll—to get back to the main topic of conversation, you're going to take Curt up on his offer the next time he gives you the chance."

"I am?"

"Definitely."

"But—"

"If you don't," Margo went on, "I'll brain you with a chair leg."

"But—"

"Look," she said, "whether or not you decide to park your shoes under his bed is something you'll have to dope out for yourself. But you're not even giving yourself a chance to decide. Go out with the guy—if nothing else, it's a free meal and a free concert."

Barbara wavered.

"Barbie," she concluded, "if you're that worried about being unfaithful to Dana that you won't go out with a guy, I think it shows something. I think it shows you don't feel too sure of yourself!"

That settled it. Even if she hadn't already decided to accept Margo's advice she would have been forced to after her last remark.

Especially because it made a certain amount of sense. Maybe she was feeling guilty about unconscious desires for another man—maybe that was the Freudian explanation for it all. But whatever it was, she wouldn't be able to look herself in the face if she had turned down Curt after what Margo had said to her.

As far as sleeping with him went—well, that was a horse of another hue entirely. At first the thought still seemed impossible even after Margo's glib words on the subject, but on second thought she even saw a certain amount of merit in a sexual relationship with Curt Tyrone. If there was no romantic bit to confuse the issue, she just might let the man make love to her.

It was hard for her to think otherwise that night as she tossed and turned in her bed. She couldn't get Margo's words out of her mind, and she saw her friend in an entirely different light now that she could picture Margo's slim, small-boned body churning under a man. As she tried to sleep her mind kept filling up with images of Margo in bed with a man, and as she came closer to dozing off Margo's face changed until it looked like her own face.

And the face of the man was Curt's.

As a result, she accepted the next invitation she got from Curt. It came less than a week later during a cigarette break in the teacher's room between fourth and fifth hour classes. Curt came into the room a second after her, just in time to light her cigarette with his silver lighter.

He asked her if she would join him for dinner and a concert two nights later.

His face didn't even change expression when she accepted the invitation.

"The concert starts at 8:30," he told her. "I'll come by for you around six so we can take our time with the dinner."

She started to give him her address but he stopped her. "I know where you live," he said. "I'll pick you up at six."

CHAPTER 4

It was Thursday and it was almost 4:30. She rushed out of the building, cursing silently at the teacher's meeting that had been called at the last minute, the meeting that had kept her at the school for more than an hour and that had, in actuality, accomplished absolutely nothing. If there was anything in the world that was duller than a teacher's meeting she had yet to discover what it was.

She hurried through the playground to her car. It was parked on Cunard and she opened the door and turned the key in the ignition without bothering to put the top down. She drove swiftly but expertly over the packed snow that was getting ready to turn to ice, drove up Parkside to Covington and to her house. Then she aimed the car up the narrow driveway and rocketed it into the garage, braking it a good half inch from the back wall.

Once she was inside the house she began to tell herself that there was no rush, that she had almost an hour and a half before he was coming for her, that if she was a minute or two late he could damn well sit down and wait for her, that there was nothing so special about him to begin with and she didn't have to knock herself out getting ready for him.

But as she was telling herself these bits of information she was simultaneously dashing up the staircase like a runaway cyclotron, tearing off her clothes as if they were infested with pubic lice, breaking the clasp of her bra in the rush and hurling the bra at a chair as if to teach it a lesson.

In the bathroom she started to run water into the tub but changed her mind after it had been running for several seconds. A bath would be a delight, a peaceful, soak-yourself-sick loll in the tub, a good hot steaming tub smelling of bubble bath. But a bath would also take time, and time was of the essence, and time was also in short supply at the moment.

Thus a shower.

She pulled the plug, watched the water as it ran down the drain and thought that water running down a drain reminded her of something. She couldn't remember what it reminded her of and decided that it wasn't the most important thing in the world, whatever it was. When all the water was gone she drew the shower curtain shut and turned on the shower, making the mixture good and hot. She grabbed a bar of soap from the sink and climbed into the tub, relaxing deep down inside the instant the spray of water hit her.

She spent a little more time under the shower than she had planned on spending. The soap was soft and it felt good to rub it over her skin, working the lather into her pores and feeling clean right through to the bone. First she washed her hair, glad that she had the kind of hair you could wash a few minutes before you went out of the house without it looking like somebody slept in it. Her hair was long and she spent a while soaping it and rinsing it, soaping and rinsing until it was squeaky clean like the television commercials.

Then she washed her face, her arms, her legs. She spent more time than was necessary soaking her breasts and belly and buttocks, taking a weird sensual delight from the experience, enjoying it all immensely. It was as if her hand with the soap in it was somebody else's hand, a hand that was teasing and caressing her. Her skin positively glowed by the time she was done.

The cold water was too much for her—she could only take it for a few seconds; then she was out of the tub and busy rubbing herself pink and dry with the big red bath towel. She brushed her teeth until she practically wore through the enamel, plucked her eyebrows neatly and precisely, shaved her legs and under her arms.

The dress she picked out was a sheath dress—an almost shocking yellow-green that fit her like a second skin. It was sexy without being obvious and she was sure he would like it. Dana, she remembered, had been very fond of it—and she had a quick pang of guilt at the memory. She forced it out of her mind.

The dress, being the type of dress it was, demanded a bra and a girdle. But, damnit, she just plain didn't feel like wearing a bra or a girdle. She compromised, wearing a bra, omitting a girdle, thinking that if the male concert goers enjoyed getting a good look at a shapely behind they would have their collective chance.

She brushed her hair and decided to wear it hanging loose instead of pinned up. It was fresh and glossy from the shower, fresh and yellow and sweet smelling. She put a dab of perfume behind each ear, painted her mouth expertly with lipstick, and put a few finishing touches upon her appearance. It was precisely five minutes to six when she was satisfied with the results and precisely six o'clock when the doorbell rang shortly and she walked downstairs to open the door and admit Curt Tyrone.

He spent a long time looking at her; then his face relaxed into a wide grin and he took her arm, leading her down the walk to his car. The car was a Plymouth with one fender battered and several years under its fan belt, and she thought automatically that Curt couldn't be earning too tremendous a living. Either that or he had better things to spend money on than a car.

They made small talk on the way to the restaurant—the usual shop talk about kids and classes. She hardly heard a word that either of them said. She was on edge. She was very much conscious of his presence on the seat beside her, very much aware of a response to the husky maleness of him. She talked easily but her mind was not on what she was saying and she wasn't sure whether or not she was making any sense as she babbled on.

The restaurant he had selected was one she had never been to before and she was glad of that much. It was just as well that they weren't eating in a place she had been to with Dana. The restaurant, called simply Cavan's, was a small brick building outside the city limits on Main Street just past Williamsville. There was a circular black bar where a few men and fewer women sat drinking; around the bar there were several tables set far apart and about a dozen booths along the walls. The headwaiter led them to a booth and she sat down across from Curt.

He ordered first and she followed his lead. They had whiskey sours first, then shrimp cocktails followed by thick blood-rare sirloins with baked potatoes. She ordered a chocolate eclair to go with her coffee; he passed up dessert and sipped a pony of brandy.

The food at Cavan's was the best restaurant meal she could remember in years. The steak was done just the way she liked it, the coffee was hot and full-bodied and rich, the shrimp in the cocktail were small and tasty and the baked potato was dripping with butter. And the atmosphere there was just as pleasant—dark walls, thick carpeting, prompt waiters, silent customers, soft music in the background that went well with the dinner without getting in the way of the conversation.

It was a place for people who liked good food in good surroundings, she thought, thinking also that that sounded like advertising copy or something. Moreover it was a place to spend a long time over dinner. Which they did.

"You're very beautiful tonight," he told her over the rim of his brandy glass. Then he put down the brandy and told her again.

"Thank you."

He said something else that she couldn't remember later and the conversation drifted away from her and how beautiful she was into more pedestrian paths. They went on talking, with a second cup of coffee appearing magically before each of them, and later she realized that although they hadn't been talking about anything much he managed to learn a good deal about her from the conversation. He was always on the receiving end of information or at least it seemed that way. He was so damned easy to talk to that she found herself unable to suppress anything.

After dinner they had to hurry to make the concert, which was only partially worth the effort. The Haydn symphony was well performed but the presence of a soprano on the program managed to kill the rest of it for her. She had never learned to enjoy a hysterical woman screeching at the top of her lungs in a foreign language.

When they were in his car again on the way home she made up her mind all at once. She had, of course, been in the process of making up her mind all evening long, but it was when he held the door open for her and helped her inside that her mind made itself up.

She would sleep with him.

It seemed only moments later when he pulled to a stop in front of her house. He got out on his side, then came around to hold the door for her and take her arm. The sky was moonless and starless and they walked up the walk to the door in absolute silence.

He waited while she fished around in her purse for the key and she wondered what he was waiting for, why he didn't take her in his arms and kiss her. She knew that he wanted to, that he wanted her as much as she wanted him if not more. But he made no move to kiss her and finally she found the key and fitted it into the lock.

She opened the door.

He still didn't try to kiss her.

She turned and looked up at him, trying to make her eyes look misty. It wasn't hard.

"I had a very nice time, Curt."

"I'm glad," he said. "So did I."

Still no kiss.

Boldly: "Would you like to come in for a drink?"

He glanced at his watch, then shook his head. "I'd better not," he said. "It's pretty late and we both have to be at school tomorrow."

Her heart sank and she was afraid that it showed on her face. What was the matter with him—didn't he want her? Or was he just too stupid to pick up his cue? Neither possibility seemed particularly likely.

"There's a good movie at the Amherst tomorrow night," he said suddenly. "I don't want you to feel that I'm giving you the rush, but would you like to see it with me?"

Now she was thoroughly confused. She told him yes, she would like very much to see the movie with him, and then he said that he'd pick her up for the movie around eight or so, that he would see her in school tomorrow, and, finally, that she should sleep well.

Then he turned, still without kissing her, and walked to his car. She opened the door and entered her house, then closed the door and hurried to the window to watch him drive off down the street.

It was hard getting to sleep that night. Her sexual desires were getting stronger than ever, fighting for control with her desire to remain true to Dana. Tonight had been a victory for sex, but it was a Pyrrhic victory in the full sense of the word—sex had won the battle but had lost the war. Dana was betrayed, mentally if not physically, and all she got out of it was a good rousing case of acute frustration. Her loins throbbed with untried passion and her brain buzzed like a machine shop.

Getting out of bed the next morning was a chore. When the alarm rang she reached groggily to shut it off but her fingers couldn't manage to find the proper button to push. The clock went on ringing its merry head off and in desperation she heaved it across the room. It caromed off a wall and made sickening sounds as the glass front shattered and small clock parts tinkled to the floor.

And, to top it off, the damned thing went on ringing. She tried pulling the covers over her head but she couldn't get rid of the sound of the clock. It seemed she had no choice but to get up. So she did, stretching like a panther and clawing the sleep from her eyes.

The house was like an icebox and she thought there was something wrong with her until it occurred to her that perhaps there was something wrong with the furnace instead. She got washed and dressed and threaded her way downstairs to stare sadly at the thermometer. It hovered in the unpleasant neighborhood of fifty-five.

She called the gas company and raised mild hell until she was finally convinced that the company could get a man over by tomorrow morning and no sooner. She told the company that if the man did not appear on schedule she would come down with pneumonia and die on their steps, a mute testimonial to the ill effects of gas heating. That seemed a comparatively good place to drop the conversation so on that note she hung up, leaving the gas company's Girl Thursday with a phone in her hand and what Barbara could guess was a puzzled expression on her face.

Breakfast was simple if only because it was too early to taste anything. She scrambled a pair of eggs and gobbled them, pouring a cup of coffee and gulped it, shivered into her overcoat and got out of the house and into her car. She was barely at school on time but she made it just under the wire and the day went by in a hurry.

She didn't run into Curt all day long. He wasn't in the lunchroom when she ate or in the teacher's room when she took a quick cigarette break. After school ended she almost went to his office looking for him but decided not to and drove straight home.

The remainder of the afternoon took longer to go by than the rest of the day had taken, or at least it seemed that way. Barbara had plenty of work to do—a stack of compositions to read and grade, a week's worth of lessons to plan, a batch of short tests to mark. She went to work at the desk in the bedroom with the papers in front of her, a red pencil in one hand, a cigarette in the other.

But she couldn't keep her mind on what she was doing. She read the same paragraph in one composition four times without having the faintest idea what she had read, and after forcing herself through the sixth straight epic entitled "Our Trip To Old Fort Niagara" she was ready to throw in the sponge. All right already—Old Fort Niagara was hell on wheels. She didn't much care.

The problem, she decided, was two-fold. First of all there was the heat, or rather the utter absence of it. She felt like going downstairs and turning off the refrigerator—there was no sense wasting electricity on it, since it was warmer inside the icebox than out of it with the furnace in its present state of inertia. She put on a sweater, then tried wearing her overcoat. It didn't help much but just made her feel a little bit bulkier.

The second part of the problem was a little more cerebral. It was Curt.

She felt all mixed-up about him, completely unsure just where she stood with him—or, for that matter, where he stood with her.

Last night she had been so ready to play bedroom games with him that she had shocked herself. Why, she was almost at the point of raping him on the front stoop, and might have if the neighborhood zoning laws hadn't frowned on such activity.

Now she was no longer sure. And she realized that her mind was probably going to change again and again until she either broke off with him entirely or wound up rolling around in the hay with him.

But how did he feel about her? It was hard to say—the guy kept so much to himself. Obviously he was interested in her or he wouldn't have asked her out a second time. But *how* was he interested—that was the question that was giving her a rough time.

If he was after her fair white body, as Margo would put it, he must have realized that a pass on the previous evening had every chance in the world of succeeding. On the other hand he was in his mid-thirties and he'd probably been around a good bit. Maybe he wanted to play a waiting game so that when he made his pass there would be virtually no chance of a refusal.

Then again, maybe his interest wasn't primarily sexual. Maybe he just wanted her company—and that, she decided, was okay too. He was fun to be with and a good escape from sitting around the house. She'd take him on those terms.

But, she thought, there was a third possibility. Mr. Curtis Tyrone just might be shopping for a wife. It was, she had to admit, more than a remote possibility—and it would explain his failure to make any attempt to sneak between her legs.

If that was the case, she was totally uninterested.

And, if that was the case, things were not working out at all.

•   •   •

She was ready at eight and he rang the bell right on time once again. She was wearing a skirt-and-sweater, the skirt a tight and simple black flannel and the sweater an equally tight and equally simple red cashmere. In a last ditch attempt to find out just where she stood with him she had omitted both bra and girdle and both her breasts and her hips moved and joggled with every step she took.

The conversation on the way to the theater was small talk again, but it was small talk with a difference. The two of them felt at home with each other now and it was almost as if they had known one another for years. She felt very comfortable sitting next to the big soft-voiced man with bright red hair—too comfortable, she told herself. She got a mental picture of the old-married-couple mood descending upon the two of them and shut her eyes hurriedly at the thought.

The picture was a foreign import from Sweden, and if any film was designed to serve as a prelude to mattress meanderings, this was the one, complete with soul-kissing and breast fondling and a nude swimming scene that had Barbara's pulse pounding vicariously. By the time they got out of the movie house her heart was hammering against her rib cage and her hands felt fluttery. She wasn't quite so shaken up that she had to hold onto Curt's arm for support, but she did anyway and he didn't seem to mind.

The night was very quiet outside, cold and clean. Curt's Plymouth was parked in the lot at the rear of the show and they walked to it in silence. Barbara let herself lean against him on the way and she bumped her behind against his hip several times accidentally on purpose. If he knew what she was doing he gave no indication of it.

"The night's young," he said when they were seated in the car. "Want to grab a few drinks? There's a nice quiet bar over on the west side."

"Sounds good. Maybe a few drinks will warm me up a little."

"Are you cold?"

She shivered. "I've been freezing all day. The damned furnace is on the fritz and the house has been like an igloo since I woke up this morning."

"Didn't you have them send a man over to fix it?"

"I called them," she said. "Evidently there's an epidemic of furnaces on the fritz. They promised to have a man come by first thing tomorrow morning."

"In that case," he said, "let's go drinking."

They went drinking. The bar, a quiet neighborhood tavern just a few blocks from the Peace Bridge, was a good place for quiet drinking. The music on the jukebox was properly pensive modern jazz and a very welcome OUT OF ORDER sign was hanging from a battered television set. Half a dozen men sat silently at the bar, most of them drinking draft beer. The bartender, a balding man with a drooping moustache and an immaculate apron that looked slightly out of place, was wiping glasses with a speckled dishrag. The part-time waitress, a faded blonde with a perpetually sad smile who doubled in brass as part-time whore, took their order and brought them drinks. Barbara had an old-fashioned; Curt drank a double shot of Irish whiskey on the rocks.

She took a sip of her drink and almost immediately felt the

alcohol reaching out for her brain with long sticky fingers. "Let's talk about you," she said impulsively. "We never talk about you."

"Don't we?"

"Never," she said. "All you do is get me to tell you my life story. I'm not one of your guidance problems, am I?"

He laughed. "I never thought of you that way, Barbara. But I guess I have been fairly non-directive."

She raised her eyebrows.

"Non-directive," he repeated. "Non-directive therapy is a technique originated by a guy named Carl Rogers. It consists of letting his client—or patient, if you prefer—lead the conversation wherever he wants. Sometimes the therapist doesn't do much more than sit on his tail waiting for the client to start talking."

"And does it work?"

"Like a charm," he said. "I don't know how good it is in actual psychoanalysis, but for my money it's the only method to use in child guidance. A kid opens up a lot more if he isn't prodded into it—and at the same time, if I sit there without saying too much on my own, without opening up paths for the kid, it makes it easier for him to get started on his own without my sidetracking him."

She didn't say anything.

"What's the matter?"

"I'm being non-directive," she explained. "Talk."

He laughed; then he talked. As he talked she began to realize how little she had known about him before, how little he had revealed to her. She finished her drink and he motioned to the broken-down blonde for another round without pausing in his conversation.

"I'm a bastard," he said, smiling when her face took on a rather strange expression. "Literally, I mean. My mother gave me to an orphanage after she had me and then disappeared off into the night. She figured she could live without me and this way somebody might give me a home.

"Somebody didn't. I wasn't the most beautiful child in the world, I guess, and prospective foster parents found better looking kids to take home with them. Then, by the time I was eleven or twelve, I didn't stand much chance of adoption any more. People want young kids—kids whose personalities they can shape to suit themselves."

He took a slug of the bourbon and stopped to look at her over the rim of the glass. Then he went on.

He told her all there was to tell or at least it seemed that way to her. Grade school at the orphanage, high school at Bishop Fallon with a job delivering papers in the morning and another job at a drugstore afternoons after school. He worked hard, hardly got any sleep nights by the time he was done studying. He wanted to save money for college but the war got in the way.

The war gave him four years walking through mud and shooting at Germans. He was in the infantry and he was a sergeant by the time the war was over. He was in Italy in time for Salerno and in France in time for the German breakthrough at the Battle of the Bulge. That was where he caught a bullet in the hip—two weeks in a hospital behind the lines and he was back fighting again.

When the war ended there was nothing to do. He felt too old for college but he didn't want to spend the rest of his life pouring steel at Bethlehem so he picked up on the GI bill and took a bachelor's degree at Niagara University. He polished off a four year course in three years and found out that psychology was an interesting enough subject for him and that he wanted to learn some more about it. A professor got him interested in guidance and he got a construction job the summer after graduation and saved up enough money to take a master's at New York University.

That, in essence, was the story. It was a story fairly empty of people—he didn't have time for deep friendships or lasting attachments. So far he'd spent most of his life walking uphill and only now, now that he was reasonably well settled in a job that he liked, could he take some time off and get his bearings on the world around him.

He told her all this in an even tone of voice, never boasting of his accomplishments or complaining about the rough breaks he had had. It was almost as though he was completing a school assignment: she had asked for the story of his life and he was giving it to her in one giant installment.

But there was more. Already a large amount of empathy had built up between them, and she knew for certain that the things he was telling her were things he had not told to many other persons. She felt much closer to him by the time he was finished.

And she decided, partially against her will, that she was beginning to like Curt Tyrone very much.

Two hours later she hated him.

Hated him like the plague.

Hated him like poison.

Hated his guts. And other vital portions of his anatomy.

Because the bastard—and he *was* a bastard—had not made the slightest attempt to warm her bed. Here she was, needing a man like a man stranded in the Sahara needs water, and here he was, dropping her at her house, giving her a silly smile, and disappearing.

It was a hell of a note.

To top it all off the house was colder than ever. She piled every blanket on top of the bed and piled clothing on top of the blankets and the bed when she got into it was still several degrees colder than Little America. She half-expected to see penguins walking around on the floor next to the bed.

The hell of it was that it didn't have to be so damned cold. If the bastard (she was beginning to think that she would always think of him as The Bastard, that she might even call him that to his face)—if he had only had the decency to crawl under the covers with her, the whole bedtime experience would have been much warmer.

She pulled the covers farther over her head and buried her face in the pillow. She knew what the bastard wanted—it wasn't hard to see that he regarded her as marriageable meat, the type of girl for a permanent type of scene.

It was ironic.

The world was filled with men who looked upon marital bliss as a blessing in the same category as gonorrhea. Such men would be happy to tumble her and very unhappy to put a ring on her finger.

She couldn't meet a man like that.

Not her.

Not with her incredible luck.

Instead, when all she wanted was a bed athlete, she had to be attracted to the one bastard in a million who had church bells ringing inside his big square head.

The bastard.

She cursed and shivered alternately, praying she would hear the bell when the cretin came in the morning to fix her fool furnace. Then she cursed and shivered some more.

For a good while she had the sneaking suspicion that she would not get to sleep until a week from next Thursday and that when she finally did get to sleep she would do a Rip Van Winkle and not wake up for a cool forty years.

A very cool forty years, with the damned furnace on the blink.

She was wrong.

She slept like a dormant dormouse and woke up instantly when the doorbell rang at 9:30.

CHAPTER 5

When the bell rang she crawled out from the warmth of the bed and stood up in the coldness of the room. She started at once for the door and even got halfway out of the bedroom before it occurred to her that it might not be good form to greet the furnace repairman without any clothes on. Even the cold last night hadn't been enough to lead her to sleep in pajamas, and now she had to hustle back into her room and grab a nightgown from the closet. She slipped it on and headed out of the bedroom and down the stairs to the front door, which she opened at once.

"You Mrs. Sussex?"

The man who wanted to know whether or not she was Mrs. Sussex, and whom she told at once that she was, was a brawny and unshaven type with a toolbox in one hand and a rather smelly corncob pipe in the other. After she had identified herself he transferred the pipe from hand to jaw and made his way inside the house.

"Gas company," he said. "Something about a furnace."

"Yes," she said. "My furnace."

"It don't work?"

"Doesn't," she said automatically, as if he was an English student of hers.

"Yeah," he said. "What I mean is there's something wrong with it."

"That's right," she said shakily. "There is."

"You want to show me where it is?"

It took her a minute to turn and lead him to the cellar stairway because she hardly was conscious of what he was saying. She saw how he was looking at her and that was enough. His eyes were like hands that carefully opened the nightgown, removed it from her shoulders, dropped it to the floor, and then began caressing her private parts.

No, she thought. Not like that. The eyes weren't that gentle. They were like hands that ripped the nightgown off her and threw her down onto the floor.

She turned then and started toward the cellar stairway. Even with her back to him she could feel the eyes burning into her, could almost feel the force of his stare on her buttocks and the backs of her thighs. The flimsy nightgown was inadequate protection.

At the head of the stairway he took off his peajacket and handed it to her, then picked up the toolbox and walked down the flight of stairs. She followed him to the cellar and pointed out the furnace, knowing as she did so that he would have no trouble finding it for himself in a cellar as empty as hers.

But she couldn't help herself. There was something frighteningly magnetic about the man and her feet followed him down the staircase without her mind being able to prevent them.

He examined the furnace like a doctor examining a patient who had every disease known to modern medicine. He shook his head very sadly and his lips turned downward.

"Wotta mess," he said. "You're lucky she didn't blow up on you."

"Can you fix it?"

"Hell," he said, "I can fix her. Haven't seen one yet I couldn't fix. She'll take some time, though. Not one of those soft jobs where you twist a lever or tighten a screw and she's all set again."

But he wasn't looking at the furnace while he said the last sentence. He was looking at Barbara.

"Take your time," she told him. She left him then and her feet were uncomfortably unsteady as she climbed the stairs.

In the kitchen she poured herself a glass of orange juice, broke two eggs into a frying pan and turned on the fire under the coffee. The orange juice she drank at once and it helped wake her up. The eggs fried happily and the coffee heated joyfully. She popped the eggs onto a plate and poured a cup full of the coffee and sat down to eat.

She was ravenous. The eggs disappeared in no time at all and were joined in short order by two slices of toast spread with butter and strawberry jam. The coffee woke her up the rest of the way and she lit a cigarette to keep it company.

She tried to think about last night.

She couldn't.

All she could think about was the man in the cellar.

Which was silly, she admitted. He was just some grubby clod of a furnace-fixer, an earthy type who probably couldn't count past four. He needed a shave and probably needed a bath as well.

So, she told herself, stop thinking about him.

She couldn't.

She took her coffee and cigarette to the living room and sat down in a chair as if the extra distance would lessen the effect the man was having upon her. If anything it had the opposite effect. She sat there rubbing her hot thighs together like a music-making cricket, knowing already what she was going to do, knowing that she did not want to do it, knowing too that she was completely powerless to prevent herself from going through with it.

The die was cast.

The cards were dealt.

The ball game was over.

After twenty minutes and two more cigarettes she couldn't sit still any longer. She stood up woodenly and walked back to the kitchen, turning on the fire again under the coffee. She waited while it heated.

When it was hot she filled two cups with it and carried them to the head of the stairway.

"I've got coffee heated," she called down to him. "Would you care for a cup?"

"That'd hit the spot. I'll be up for it in a minute."

"Never mind coming up—I'll bring it down to you."

She brought both cups of coffee down to the cellar. He turned to take the coffee and she was illogically glad to see a half-hidden expression of puzzlement on his face. He wasn't sure exactly what she was up to and she was pleased. He'd find out soon enough.

Then his eyes rested once again on the front of her nightgown and the shadow of a smile replaced the puzzled look.

He took the coffee from her and sat down on the cold cellar floor with it. "Damn fine coffee," he said.

She took a sip of her own coffee.

He looked up at her. "Sure nice of you," he said. "Lots of women won't take the trouble to bring a guy a cup of coffee."

"It just seemed the decent thing to do."

"Yeah, sure. But most dolls don't think to take the time from whatever else they're doing. They don't realize how cold it gets in a cellar on a day like this."

"It's very cold, isn't it?"

He stood up, draining the coffee cup. "Yeah," he said. "Damn cold. Good thing I got something to warm me up. The coffee, I mean."

He was almost as subtle as a bomb and for a minute she was angry with him. Then she decided that it was better that he wasn't subtle, wasn't clever—that he was just an animal for the performance of a function that was basically animalistic. She let herself smile.

His eyes grew bolder.

Dana, she thought. *Forgive me, Dana. Forgive me for I know precisely what I do.*

And I can't help it.

Dana, forgive me.

And she let the nightgown fall open.

Her face was expressionless. She simply stood there with her body completely exposed to him without a thought in her head or a feeling in her body other than acute physical hunger.

His face, on the other hand, was not at all expressionless.

His mouth hung open.

At least, she thought, he didn't waste time talking. He stood up at once and stood very still for a moment just staring at her and letting his eyes warm her up.

Then he came closer.

She didn't move at all while he took the few steps that brought him next to her. She didn't offer any resistance when his hand came out and held her breast like a piece of ripe fruit.

He let go of her breast and reached to catch her long hair in his hand. He held it too tightly and it hurt her. Then he pulled at her hair and her head came forward to meet his. Their mouths met and her mouth was open at once as his lips ground painfully against her. His tongue probed her mouth like an unknown intruder and she fell against him, the harsh fabric of his overalls rough against her bare skin.

When he released her she fell forward toward him and he took her in his arms with his hands on her shoulders and kissed her again, harder than before. He bit her lips and she felt the blood beginning to flow from them.

He pushed the nightgown back from her shoulders and she lowered her arms so that it fell to the floor. He kicked it away impatiently and all she could think of was that the poor nightgown would be horribly dirty.

His hands dropped from her shoulders and cupped her tight buttocks, pressing her against him. She clung to him, taut against him from head to toe, wanting him desperately, wanting him and hating both him and herself at the same time.

His grip tightened upon her buttocks.

God, she thought. *God, he's going to kill me.*

"Upstairs?"

She shook her head.

"Where?"

"Here."

He let go of her and stared at her. "Here?"

She nodded, unable to speak.

"It's filthy."

"I don't care."

"But—"

"*Come on!*"

He didn't take off his shoes or socks, and she thought fleetingly that he looked quite ridiculous standing there in his shoes and socks with no other clothes on.

Then he reached for her again.

He took her in his arms and the sudden contact of flesh on flesh was too much for her. A little scream tore from her throat, a little scream that was a product of all the nights in a lonely bed, all the hungers that she had had no way of satisfying.

She was limp as a soggy noodle as he lowered her to the floor. He lay down beside her, his hands reaching for her breasts, tightening upon them and sending urgent stabs of pain through her whole body.

Her back and buttocks scraped against the cold basement floor. His breath was foul in her face and his fingers dug into her shoulders. She closed her eyes and wanted to scream her lungs out.

Then nothing mattered, nothing but the simple physical union of man and woman. It was agony—but an agony she craved, an agony she couldn't possibly have gone on living without.

At the climax his teeth closed on the side of her throat.

She shrieked.

Then it was over.

When he drew away from her and fumbled his way into his clothes she lay inert on the frigid floor. She felt as though she was covered from head to toe with goat manure. She wanted to die.

"That was nice," he said. "You got a pretty good body there and you sure know how to use it."

She couldn't say anything. She just wished that he would shut up and leave her alone.

"Don't your husband mind when you play games like this? Or don't he know about it?"

Oh, God, she thought. Aloud she said: "My husband's dead."

"Yeah? Well, you widows sure know what to do when you got a man on top of you."

Leave me alone.

"I guess you get all hot and bothered living alone. Must be rough until a guy like me comes along."

Just leave me alone.

He finished dressing and started up the staircase. She was glad to see him going; then, hysterically, she realized that he hadn't fixed the furnace yet. Just as he reached the top step she called to him.

"Aren't you going to . . . to finish the furnace?"

He laughed coarsely.

"Lady," he said, turning to look at her again, "all it needed was a five-minute job. I was finished with her a long while before you came down with that coffee."

She opened her mouth, then closed it. She understood.

But he had to drive the point home anyway. "I knew what you were looking for," he said. "I figured a piece of something nice like you might be worth waiting around for. Turned out I was right. Maybe I'll drop around again one of these days and give you another good boffing. We can use the bed next time—the floor's all right now and then, but—"

"Don't come back!"

He was putting on his peajacket now and he looked up to laugh at her again.

"Maybe I will," he said. "And maybe I won't. Depends whether or not I decide you're worth it."

Then, mercifully, he was gone.

She remained where she was for several minutes. Then she discovered that she was going to be violently ill at any moment and raced naked up the stairs to the bathroom on the first floor. She got there just in time and her stomach turned inside out until she was too weak to stand up.

There goes my breakfast, she thought hysterically. *I ought to fry a couple more eggs and make some more toast. But for some strange reason I don't feel like eating anything, not just now. Maybe in a little while . . .*

She lit a cigarette but it tasted foul and she stubbed it out after the first puff. After a minute or two she went back to the cellar to stuff the soiled nightgown into the hamper. Then she changed her mind—she could never bring herself to wear the gown again no matter how many times she washed it, so she took it from the hamper and wadded it into a ball and deposited it in the garbage can.

She managed to drag herself upstairs. She ran water into the tub as hot as she could stand it and soaked in the tub for four hours until she was waterlogged. Then she took a scalding shower, soaping and rinsing and soaping and rinsing until her skin was ready to come off in handfuls.

She still felt filthy.

Finally she got out of the tub and dried herself gently with the towel. Back in her bedroom she dressed quickly, not because she was going anywhere but because she didn't want to be naked anymore. She sat down in the chair next to her bed and lit another cigarette, trying without too much success to be calm and relaxed.

She was still unsure just how she felt about what had happened that morning. She was desperately ashamed of herself, sick of herself and of him, nauseous at the memory of what the pair of them had done. And what did she have for her troubles? A momentary orgasm which had more than worn off by now, bruises on her shoulders and throat and thighs, soreness in her breasts, and a hideous sick feeling centered in the pit of her stomach.

The shame overshadowed everything. What was she—an animal? A bitch in heat? A throbbing vagina with a body attached to it?

And yet, along with all the feelings of revulsion, there was the knowledge that the experience had been necessary in its own way, that it brought no emotional involvement and that it would never be repeated. The grimy sadist would never be her lover again, in spite of his vague "promise" to return.

And she might even be able to take another lover again sometime in the future. She knew now that Margo had been perfectly right: a woman like her could not live a sexless life. Sometime she might meet another man, someone who could take her on a purely physical plane without humiliating her the way . . . the way—

She didn't know whether to laugh or to cry when she realized that she didn't even know the man's name.

A few cigarettes later the phone rang. It was Margo.

"Hi," she said. "How was your date?"

"All right."

"Just all right? Did he make a pass?"

"No," she said dully. "He didn't make a pass."

"What if he had?"

She dodged the question.

"I was luckier last night," Margo informed her. "I had just what I wanted."

She didn't know exactly how to sidetrack the conversation, and although she wanted nothing less at that moment than a full and precise description of Margo's sexual acrobatics, that was just what she got. Blow-by-blow, kiss-by-kiss, caress-by-caress.

Margo had evidently had one hell of a time.

"Hell," Margo said finally, "I must be working you up something awful, you poor kid. Look, do you want to drop by for dinner tonight?"

She didn't.

"I'm sorry, Margo. I'm busy."

"You seeing Curt? Has the fabulous Mr. Tyrone got a date with Our Gal Barbie tonight?"

"No," she said. "Just a stack of compositions I want to clear out of the way."

"They suddenly can't wait until tomorrow?"

"I'd rather get to them tonight, Margo."

"You're sure it's all work and no play? You're not crossing me up and getting laid tonight, are you?"

She had to laugh in spite of herself. She assured Margo that she was just spending her time at home and managed to end the conversation.

Then Curt called minutes later.

"Barbara? How about dinner tonight?"

"Not tonight," she said. "I've got a lot of work to get finished with."

"You're sure?"

"Positive."

"Okay then," he said. "Everything all right?"

"Yes—why?"

"I don't know—you sound a little bit shaky."

"Everything's all right," she assured him. "I'll see you Monday."

Everything wasn't all right.

After dinner—which she ate about a third of and which she

didn't taste—she tried to read a book and listen to a Boccherini cello sonata.

Both attempts failed. The book didn't make any sense and the music floated past her without registering. She put the book back in the bookcase and turned off the hi-fi, returning to her room to get the schoolwork out of the way.

Surprisingly she worked very efficiently. Like a robot, she thought. A pencil in one hand and a cigarette in another, correcting grammar and construction and handing out grades and outlining lessons without giving one little whoop in hell about the whole routine.

A robot.

Get the all-purpose Barbara Sussex robot, she thought dizzily. It walks, it talks, it wets its pants. It teaches infants how to read and write, it holds stimulating conversations with stimulating people, and it goes through life with the enthusiasm and intelligence of a papier-mâché whale.

And it fornicates, she added. Mustn't forget that. It fornicates like a bunny on a diet of Spanish Fly.

Softly she warbled:

Fornication hits the spot
Give the pastime all you've got
Sleep and sleep until you're blue
Fornication is the thing for you . . .

It was only a quarter after eight when she was finished with her work. She made another stab at book-and-Boccherini and failed miserably. Then she knew what it was she wanted to do.

The vodka bottle was two-thirds full.

More than enough.

Vodka, she thought as she tilted the bottle, was the only sensible way to get alcohol into the bloodstream. Vodka, she thought as she filled the water tumbler half full, was a perfect medium for getting blissfully fried without having to taste liquor. Vodka, she thought as she added the orange juice, was a friend in need. Add it to orange juice and it was like drinking orange juice. Add it to prune juice and it was like drinking prune juice, if you happened to flip over that type of scene.

Vodka, she thought as she drank a third of the glassful in one monstrous swallow, was a blessing, the dearest companion of the Robotic Fornicator.

After the first glass she drank more slowly but very steadily. She didn't get the least bit high, never at all giddy or giggly.

She simply got drunk.

The alcohol worked on her like an anesthetic. She drank and things didn't matter. She drank and the morning seemed less horrible and the future less dreadful to contemplate. She drank and the world took on a neutral coloring of dove grey that was easier on the nervous system than the brighter colors.

By eleven she had done enough drinking. She was still steady on her feet and her mind still functioned but the unpleasant images had been dispelled and life was palatable if not delectable. She mounted the stairs slowly, undressed slowly, and slowly got into bed.

Her last conscious thought was comforting.

At least the day had not been a total loss. Something, she told herself, had been accomplished.

Something very vital.

The furnace was fixed.

CHAPTER 6

Vodka, she thought the next morning as she rubbed sleep from clear eyes, was a blessing. Vodka did not leave you with a hangover.

She awoke a little after ten and went downstairs for breakfast fully dressed. She was hungry, especially after the little she had eaten the previous day, and she made short work of four eggs and three slices of toast. The first cup of black coffee went nicely with the first cigarette, and the pair was followed by another cup of coffee and another cigarette. Then, with the business of waking up taken care of, she was ready to face the fact that it was Sunday.

There was, first of all, the regular ritual of Sunday to be observed. Accordingly she left the house and backed the car out of the driveway, then drove to the nearest drugstore on Hertel Avenue where she bought the Sunday edition of the New York *Times*. She drove back home and sat down with the paper in the living room, beginning the task of reading it. While she rarely managed to get through all of the local morning paper in the course of the day, she always read almost all there was to read of the Sunday *Times*.

She started with the book review section, then knocked off the theatrical section and the music reviews, then the news of the week in review, and finally, when there was nothing much else left of the paper, the sports section and the financial pages. These last two topics were about as interesting to her as a report on comparative annual rainfall in the Gobi and Sahara deserts, but Dana had managed to convince her in the course of their marriage that a thorough reading of the Sunday *Times* was an absolute essential.

She was a quick reader and she went through the paper rapidly. Her mind didn't wander from what she was reading and she knew that the vodka had done precisely the job for which it was intended. She wasn't depressed any more. She felt fine.

So, when Curt called her a few minutes after four in the afternoon, she was more than willing to talk with him. She was pleased that he had called, and the interlude she had spent with the nameless repairman the other morning didn't bother her any longer.

"Barbara?"

"What is it, Curt?"

"How are you feeling?"

"Fine—why?"

"You seemed a little blue last night."

"Well, everything's fine now."

"How about dinner?"

She considered. She could think of a dozen reasons offhand for telling him that she was busy but they seemed very immaterial all at once. What was important, she decided, was the fact that she wanted to have dinner with him.

Which seemed like enough of a reason.

"Dinner sounds like a good idea, Curt."

"Six-thirty okay?"

"Fine," she said.

Then something occurred to her.

"Curt—"

"Yes?"

"Curt, I don't much feel like going out for dinner tonight. Why don't you come over and let me cook you a meal?"

He hesitated.

"I mean it," she said. "I haven't cooked for anybody but myself since . . . Dana died. You don't want me to let myself get rusty, do you?"

"Well—"

"Come on over about six-thirty," she finished. "I'll have a meal ready for you that'll beat anything the restaurants have to offer."

He laughed. "You talked me into it. Will six-thirty give you enough time?"

"Plenty of time. Dinner's not going to be *that* fancy, you know."

He told her he'd be on time and she waited until he hung up. Then she replaced the receiver in its cradle and walked back to the living room, humming softly to herself. She felt very good all of a sudden, very pleased with herself and very happy that Curt was coming for dinner. She was looking forward to it.

There were four lamb chops in the freezer and she decided that they would do nicely. She put potatoes in the oven to bake, thawed out a package of chopped spinach and got it cooking with a can of cream of mushroom soup. She hadn't been bragging when she told him she would do better than the restaurants—she was an excellent cook and this was the first real cooking she had done since Dana died.

While she was setting the table in the dining room she found herself getting the first guilt pangs over the whole idea. She had managed to rationalize going out with Curt and could even think of herself sleeping with him, but now that she thought about it, cooking dinner for him seemed wrong in some unexplainable way. It was as if the intimacy they would be sharing was an intimacy that should be reserved for a husband, for Dana.

And it could have only unfavorable results with Curt. He couldn't help thinking that she wanted their relationship to develop along permanent lines. If she specifically made the point of asking him over for dinner, how could he help thinking she wanted him as a husband?

It was a definite problem.

But what could she do about it?

She put her hand to her forehead and tried to concentrate. She was going about everything ass-backward, she told herself. She couldn't just keep groping her way around, torturing herself constantly and winding up doing things that only made her feel guilty afterwards. Little sidelines like the affair with the furnace goon, whatever his name might be, were definitely not the answer to her problems. Neither was the type of involvement which was developing between her and Curt.

So—

So, she thought, what she had to do was to decide once and for all just what sort of a deal she wanted for herself. Then she could go out and get it. If she could straighten her own mind out everything would be a lot easier.

Okay.

In that case, what did she want?

Marriage?

That wouldn't be hard to get. Curt wanted her, and with a little response from her he'd probably have a ring on her finger within a month at the most. And Curt would be as good a husband as she could possibly want. He was as nice a man as she knew, as attractive a man as she knew, as good a man as she knew.

There was only one thing wrong with him.

He was not Dana.

Marriage to Curt might be nice, might be good for her. But it was a luxury she could not permit herself, a luxury which would require her to become Curt's wife instead of Dana's widow. Above all else she wanted to remain true to Dana.

So marriage was out.

Okay—there was another alternative. She could live the life she had started to lead, a life of celibacy. She could cut off her ties with Curt, avoid seeing any other men, and prepare herself for a life of solitary slumber. In time she might even find herself getting used to it.

But that was no good either.

Sooner or later she would find a man—possibly in the same horrible way that she had found a man the day before. She would be trying to stay pure and then, when her body got the best of her mind, she would feel like pulling her fingernails out by the roots.

So celibacy was out.

Now what in the world did that leave?

The answer, at this point, was obvious—so obvious that it seemed to have a string attached to it somewhere. She took a long time thinking about it, but strangely enough she couldn't find the string. Either there was no string there or it was too well hidden for her to find it.

Simple answer.

She would have an affair with Curt.

That would do it; it would solve everything, at least for the time being. He wanted her and she wanted him, and if the two of them had each other they would both be happy as a result. She would set the stage—dinner for two, candlelight, music on the hi-fi and wine with the meal. There was a bottle of Beaujolais in the cellar that hadn't been opened; it would be perfect with the chops.

Then, if Curt didn't come right out and make a pass, she would arrange the situation so that he couldn't help himself. She could even pretend to be a little tipsy from the wine and make fairly obvious overtures to him without looking cheap while she was doing it. Then the two of them would wind up in bed and that would be the ballgame.

She smiled. She hurried down the cellar stairs, only feeling momentarily sick when she remembered what had gone on a day ago in that same cellar. Then she had the wine bottle in her hand and she was up the stairs again and out of the cellar and she felt fine once more.

It would be good, she decided.

Better than good.

Wonderful.

In fact, if she had to, she could even close her eyes and pretend it was Dana.

     •   •   •

Dinner was a howling success.

That was putting it mildly. Curt was on time, as she knew he would be, and she took his coat and hung it on a hanger in the hall closet. Then, when she led him into the small dining room and switched off the overhead light, the two red candles flickered bravely and cast an intimate glow over the table.

"This is lovely," he said.

She didn't say a word.

The food was all ready and she began serving. She filled both their plates in the kitchen and brought them out. Then, silently, she handed him the Beaujolais and a corkscrew. He opened the bottle and poured wine for both of them.

It was delicious.

So, for that matter, was the food.

The wine bottle was half empty by the time they were finished with dinner. He had drunk somewhat more of it than she had, but she had had enough so that she was beginning to feel the effects of it. When she carried their empty plates into the kitchen she stopped to glance at her reflection in the hall mirror. Her eyes were shining with more brilliance than usual and her complexion was rosy. She smiled at the mirror, looking for all the world like a woman waiting with open arms for a man to come along and seduce her.

Which was precisely what she was.

"Let's kill the wine in the living room," she suggested. "It'll be more comfortable in there and I can put some music on."

"Fine idea."

He stood up and she led the way. While she was putting a record on the turntable he sat down in the easy chair. She picked out something to set the mood—a Mendelssohn sonata for cello and piano that was properly subdued and properly romantic. It was the perfect sort of thing for a seduction, she thought. The interplay between the low-keyed cello and the higher piano was like the love play of a man and a woman, which was precisely what she wanted to develop.

"Don't sit there," she told him. She walked to the couch and sat down.

"Where do you want me?"

She patted the couch beside her. "Right here," she said. "Next to me."

With a smile he joined her on the couch. She handed him one of the glasses—she didn't know or much care which was his and which was hers—and he filled them both with the wine. She flashed a soft smile and touched her glass to his. They drank.

"What's that playing?"

She told him.

"It's nice," he said. "I like Mendelssohn."

"So do I."

"In fact," he went on, "I like this whole evening. You were right—you cooked a better meal than any chef in town."

"I'm glad you liked it."

"And the wine," he added, taking a sip of his to prove his point, "is better than anything we'd have run up against."

She didn't say anything.

"And the atmosphere is perfect. You know, I've never been alone with you before this. It's kind of nice to sit across a table from you without a roomful of people around."

"That's what I thought. I didn't feel like running around tonight. I thought a nice quiet dinner at home might be fun."

"You were certainly right. I . . . haven't had anything like this in a long time, Barbara. Too long. It's a good change to sit like this with a woman like you."

She said a silent prayer of thanks to the food, the candlelight, the wine and the music. The conversation was going in just the direction she wanted and she moved a little closer to him on the couch.

"Why don't you take off your jacket, Curt? You'd be more comfortable without it."

"Good idea." He stood up and took off the sport jacket, hanging it over the back of a chair. Then he was sitting beside her again.

She finished her wine. He drained his glass and filled them both again. After they clinked glasses once more and she took a little sip of the wine she was beginning to feel the effects of it.

It made her want him more than ever.

She turned to him and looked into his eyes. "This is nice," he said again, his eyes serious. "It's a pleasure to sit on a couch with a beautiful woman."

"Like me?"

"Like you. You're a very beautiful woman, Barbara."

Her eyes twinkled. "For a guidance counsellor," she said, "you're overplaying your role."

"What do you mean?"

"I mean you're being too damned non-directive."

"Am I?"

She nodded.

"What should I do?"

Her lips parted slightly and she let her eyelids drop half shut. She took a deep breath and let it out slowly while he waited for her to speak.

Finally she said: "You just might try kissing me."

He didn't need a second invitation. He smiled and reached for her and she went into his arms at once, glad he was there, glad his arms were around her, glad his mouth was there to kiss her. He kissed her very gently at first and the kiss was just a brief meeting of two pairs of lips, just a quick and very chaste kiss before his mouth moved away from hers and her head was pressed tight against his chest.

"Barbara—"

"Don't talk," she said. "Kiss me again."

He took the tip of her chin in one hand and raised her mouth to meet his. The kiss started out the same as the first one—gentle and proper.

That's not how it ended.

Her arms went around him and she pressed herself against him, hard. Her mouth opened and she forced her tongue between his lips, probing, seeking his, inflaming him. The boldness of her kiss seemed to startle him but only for a minute. Then he was responding eagerly, returning the kiss with full passion, his arms tightening into steel bands around her soft body and his tongue tasting the sweet wine-taste of her mouth.

The kiss was not over for quite awhile. When he released her at last her eyes were shining as if they had been given a coat of oil and her heart was beating at a much faster tempo than the music that was still playing.

"You must think I'm shameless," she said. "Kissing you like that."

He didn't say anything.

"I don't care," she said. "I don't care what you think. I wanted you to kiss me that way. I want you, Curt. I don't want to play games. I think we're both old enough so that we don't have to play games."

He nodded.

"So I'm not going to play games any more," she said firmly. "I'm going to take what I want. I don't give a damn what anybody thinks any more."

He stroked the side of her cheek and she pressed her face against the palm of his hand, thinking how good and how strong he was, how much she wanted him.

"Now you're the one who's talking too much," he said.

"I am?"

He didn't answer her. Instead he took her face between his two big hands and kissed her again, kissed her deeply and thoroughly, kissed her until her head was swimming and her heart was racing, kissed her again and again until she couldn't stand it any longer, couldn't take another minute of it. She needed him, needed him more than she had needed anybody in a long, long time.

When he released her she stood up.

"Come on," she said.

He stood up, taking her hand in his. She thought fleetingly that she ought to take the record off the machine, then decided that it would shut itself off and there were more important matters to take care of first.

"Where are we going?"

"Upstairs," she said. "Come on."

As they walked to the bedroom she couldn't help comparing what was happening with what had happened the day before, couldn't help contrasting Curtis Tyrone to the man whose name she did not know. It was so much better this way, so much cleaner and so much more correct. And it would be better, much better.

Her feelings for Curt were so much different, to begin with. She liked him, liked him very much, while the furnace repairman had been just a means to an end, just a walking talking masturbatory device. This was different—this was an experience two people would share, a giving and taking that wouldn't be followed by overwhelming revulsion the instant after orgasm.

When they were in the bedroom with the door shut behind them she turned to him and he took her in his arms. They kissed and it was magic, true magic, and their bodies seemed ready to melt together.

They sat down together on the edge of the bed and he kissed her again, his hand finding her breast and holding it gently, magically, holding her and handling her so tenderly and at the same time so wonderfully that she thought she would explode. She wasn't wearing a bra and she could feel his fingers very easily through the thin material of her sweater.

When he let go of her she stood up and pulled the sweater over her head. Then she sat down again and his warm hands on her bare flesh were driving her out of her mind.

His hand slipped under her skirt and touched her knee. He

kissed her again and his hand moved higher along the inside of her thigh where the skin was even softer. When his fingers stroked the skin there it was sheer, ecstatic torture for her and she couldn't breathe.

His fingers moved higher.

Higher.

His touch through the sheer silk of her brief panties was unbearably exciting.

He didn't take her right away. Neither of them could help making the love play last as long as it possibly could and he took time to touch her and kiss her everywhere, with each caress building her passion to a higher peak.

Then, when another second's delay would have been too much, they were together.

And then the whole earth disappeared and the noise went away and they were left completely alone with each other, alone and together.

"Barbara—"

"Don't talk," she whispered. "Not now. Not for another minute or two."

She was lying in his arms with her head on his shoulder, at peace at last, at peace with him and with herself, lying in his arms and smelling the sweet acrid man-smell of him. It was as if she had just now rediscovered what relaxation was; she couldn't have moved just then if her life had depended on it.

Fortunately, it didn't.

Then he said: "You're wonderful, Barbara."

"No, I'm not. I'm not wonderful at all."

"I think you are."

"I'm not wonderful. I'm a cheap little tramp who got you over here for the express purpose of getting you to bed with me. I'm a little slut."

He didn't say anything.

"And you know what? I don't give a damn if I'm a slut. I just don't care, Curt. This is too . . . too good for me to worry about it."

He kissed her. "You're not a slut," he said. "You're the most perfect woman in the world."

She smiled softly.

"Tell me about me," she said.

"To begin with, you're beautiful."

"What's beautiful about me?"

"Everything."

"For example?"

"Your face, your eyes, your lips, the way you walk—everything."

"How about these?"

"Magnificent," he said.

"And this?"

"Too magnificent to describe."

"Aren't you going to kiss it?"

He kissed it.

"Curt—"

"What, darling?"

"Will you . . . make love to me again tonight?"

He chuckled. "Coax me."

She did better than that.

She kissed him.

He sighed and pushed her down on the bed. "You've coaxed me," he said. "That's enough coaxing."

He kissed her and all at once she was a thing of fire again, ready for him, needing him. Her arms tightened around him and she ran her hands over his broad back.

Then she thought of something.

"Curt—"

He waited for her.

"Curt, I want to ask you a favor."

"Go ahead."

She took a breath. "Curt, I don't want you to be here when I wake up in the morning. I . . . I want to be alone. Do you understand?"

"I think so."

"Is that . . . is it all right?"

"If that's what you wanted."

She could detect an edge of disappointment in his voice. "Kiss me," she said. "Kiss me again."

He kissed her.

"Touch me."

He touched her.

"Do everything to me."

He did everything to her.

CHAPTER 7

When she woke up the next morning alone in bed she said a quick silent prayer of thanks to Curt. She needed to be alone, needed to wake up by herself rather than with a man in bed beside her. She got out of bed a second or two after the alarm rang, showered quickly and dressed quicker, gobbling down a fast breakfast and packing her notes and papers in her briefcase.

It was a perfect morning. There was snow on the ground but not much of it and the sun was shining in a cloudless sky. It was a natural morning to walk to work, so she left the car in the garage and walked the few blocks to the school with her briefcase under her arm.

She felt wonderful. Standing in the classroom, talking to the children, passing out papers and working her way through the material of the day, she felt even better. She was glad to be alive, really glad now, and it made a difference.

Margo noticed the difference. They were alone in the teacher's room between third and fourth hour—she still hadn't seen Curt—and Margo winked at her. It was an extremely knowing wink.

And Barbara blushed.

"Well," said Margo, her lips curling into a smile. "So you finally crossed the bridge."

'What bridge?"

"I was speaking metaphorically. You know what a metaphor is, don't you? Hell, you're an English teacher. You have to teach the little morons all there is to know about metaphors and similes and all, don't you?"

She nodded, puzzled.

"So," Margo went on, "what I'm getting at is that you finally went out and got yourself banged good and proper."

"*How did you—*"

Margo laughed. "Nobody sent me a telegram, if that's what you're worrying about. Honey, anybody with a brain could tell that you didn't sleep alone last night. God, it shows in your face. You're so damned starry-eyed and rosy you look like either a planetarium or a garden, I'm not sure which. Who was the lucky guy?"

Her mouth opened but she didn't say anything.

"C'mon—don't keep Margo in the dark. Just because some son of a gun is keeping *you* in the dark is no reason for you to do the same for me. Of course, maybe he isn't keeping you in the dark. Maybe you make love with the lights on, for all I know. That's your business. But I would like to be able to find out—"

"It was Curt," she broke in.

Margo's eyebrows rose.

"I—"

"Well," said Margo. "Well, well, well."

"Well?"

"Very well. Congratulations, kitten. I'm real proud of you. Is he as good as he looks?"

She reddened.

"Well, I'll be triple-damned. You're blushing, kitten! He must be the hottest thing since Hell."

"Margo—"

The brunette winked again and ducked her ashes in the ashtray. "Look," she said, "I don't want to get on your nerves or anything. I just want you to know that I'm proud of you and I'm not kidding when I say it. You're a good kid, Barbara."

"Thank you."

Margo reached over and took her hand. "Never worry," she said. "You're doing the right thing and there's nothing to worry about. You're a woman, kitten. You can't hide it, you know."

"That's what I decided."

"Good girl." She winked again. "Gotta go," she announced. "Carry on, kitten. Keep those bed springs squeaking."

She saw Curt in the lunchroom but there was no way for them to get off by themselves. They shared a table instead with an old maid kindergarten teacher and another older woman and kept their conversation on an annoyingly impersonal plane. This irritated Barbara—she was anxious to get Curt off by himself, to talk to him. They had a lot of things to talk about, a lot of points to straighten out. But she didn't think the other teachers would fit very well into the type of conversation she had in mind.

She had to wait until school was over for the day. The afternoon classes went somewhat slower than the morning ones had but finally school was out for the day, with the last little brat sent on his way and the last bit of chalk wiped from the blackboard.

She struggled into her coat, locked her homeroom and headed for the door.

As if by prearrangement she met Curt on the front steps and he took her arm at once, leading her across the playground to his car.

"I want to talk to you," he said.

"That makes us even. I want to talk to you myself."

"Here?"

"We can go to my house."

He thought for a minute. "How about my apartment? We've never been to my apartment."

"We've only been to my house once. I wouldn't want you to forget what it's like."

"I strongly doubt that I'll forget it," he said. "It made a fairly deep impression on me."

"Just the house?"

"You, too. C'mon—let me show you the apartment."

"I don't know," she teased. "I might be compromised if I went alone to a bachelor's apartment."

"Oh?"

She nodded emphatically. "Besides," she added, "I'm not sure I know you well enough."

He tangled his fingers in her long hair and drew her face close to his. She didn't protest when he kissed her. Then, after he kissed her a second time, she drew away from him.

"Not here," she said.

"Why not?"

"This close to the school? Some of the kids might see us."

"So what? I believe in giving kids a liberal education."

"This liberal?"

"Why not?"

She grinned. "In that case," she said, "we might as well get in the back seat and give them a real show for their money while we're at it."

He laughed. "Enough of this," he said. "We're going to my apartment."

And they went to his apartment.

His apartment was located in a residential hotel on Franklin Street fairly far downtown. He could have gotten a place closer to school and cheaper, but the hotel had a large parking lot and was close to all the downtown stores and theaters, and more important guaranteed that his bed would be made and his room straightened up every day. It was a nice place—small but comfortable, with one room plus a tiny kitchenette and a private bathroom. Although the hotel had supplied the furnishings, the place had the unmistakable imprint of Curtis Tyrone on it. The prints on the walls were obviously ones that he had chosen; the absence of any kitchen paraphernalia other than a pot for boiling water, a coffee cup, a teaspoon and a jar of instant coffee, indicated that the occupant of the apartment was a man—and one who didn't like to cook much for himself.

"Can I sell you a drink?"

"This early in the afternoon? You'll corrupt me."

"Scotch or bourbon?"

"Whatever you're having."

She sat down in a chair while he mixed bourbon highballs. He brought her her drink and sat down in the chair next to her. They clinked glasses and sipped their drinks.

"I want to talk to you," he said.

"I'm listening."

"It's hard to tell just where to start." He scratched his head, then took out a cigarette for himself and gave her one. He lit them and they smoked and drank in silence for a moment.

"Barbara, you asked me to leave before you woke up. Why didn't you want me to stay with you?"

She shrugged.

"Tell me."

She took a deep breath and let it out slowly. Then she said: "I'm not sure."

"Any idea?"

She didn't answer.

"Let me try another tack. Where do you want our relationship to go?"

She thought that one over.

"Do you want to marry me?"

She closed her eyes and shook her head from side to side.

"That's what I thought," he said. "And you're afraid that I'll try to persuade you to marry me?"

She hesitated, then nodded.

"Do you love me?"

She opened her eyes now and looked at him. She started to say *No* instantly; then she changed her mind and just stared.

"I don't know," she said.

"How do you feel about me?"

"I like you very much, Curt. You know that already. I like to be with you and to talk to you and to . . . to make love with you. But you know that already."

He nodded.

"Curt, I don't . . . I don't want anything permanent. I don't want to love—can you understand what I'm saying?"

"Partially."

"I don't want to— Curt, I was married. You know that."

"I know."

"And I loved my husband. I still love him. He's dead, but I love him and I'm going to go on loving him."

"Of course."

"And—"

"And that means you don't want to love anybody else in the meantime?"

She thought about what he had said. "Yes," she said finally. "I guess that's it, Curt. I want you, and I want to . . . well, to have an affair with you. That makes it sound awfully mechanical and I don't want it to sound that way, but I think you can understand what I'm trying to say."

"I think so. You want closeness without any strings attached."

She nodded gratefully.

He finished his drink and put the glass down on the table next to him. "Barbara," he said, "I like you very much. I think I'm in love with you, although I'm not sure just what that's supposed to mean. I'd like to marry you, and I'd like to spend the rest of my life loving you."

She didn't say anything. She waited for him to go on.

"I think I can understand what's been going through your mind," he went on. "My natural reaction is to try to argue you out of it—I suppose that's automatic. I'm not going to, not now at any rate. Whatever you wind up deciding is your business. You can call the shots for now."

"All right."

"I'd like for us to see each other as much as possible," he said. "I'd like for us to live together, but I suppose that would be too much like marriage."

"I think so."

"When we sleep together," he said, "I'd like to spend the whole night with you. I'd like to wake up with you there next to me. But we can let that wait awhile, until you're ready for it. I don't want to force you into anything."

"Good. I . . . I appreciate this, Curt."

He smiled; then his eyes went very serious and he took a long look at her. She finished her drink, wondering what he was going to do next, and then he stood up and walked over to her.

She stared up at him.

He bent over and his hands fastened on her upper arms. He lifted her and she came up from the chair and into his arms. He kissed her and her mouth opened for him and her body pressed tight against him from head to toe. Desire welled up within her and when the kiss ended she had to lean against him for support.

He began to unbutton her dress. The dress buttoned down the back and she leaned limp against him with her firm breasts pressing into his chest while he eased the buttons out of the buttonholes.

"We've got a lot of work to do," he said.

"Work?"

"Sure. We've got a lot to find out about each other."

"We do?"

"Uh-huh."

He slipped the dress over her shoulders and it fell to the floor. She didn't move but stood like a statue in her bra and panties with the dress down around her knees.

"A lot of work," he repeated. "Since we'll only be spending a certain amount of time together, we have to make the most of that time. Right?"

"Right."

"And for that reason—"

He dropped the bra and pulled his shirt loose from his pants, unbuttoned it and took it off. Then he was pulling her close to him again and her breasts were firm and soft against his chest.

"Come on," he said. "We've got to do some basic research." He took her hand and led her to the bed. He pushed back the covers and picked her up in his arms, placed her gently in bed and climbed in alongside.

"Like this."

"Oooooh!"

He began to caress her in a way she had never been caressed before, never in her entire life, a way she had never even dreamed of, and she couldn't control herself any more.

"Oh Curt! You're wonderful! Wonderful!"

"Barbara—"

"Oh, don't stop. Don't stop, don't ever stop . . . don't stop . . ."

CHAPTER 8

"I never see you any more," Margo complained. "Where have you been spending all your time?"

"Guess."

"I think I can guess. You know, it'll get sore if you don't give it a chance to rest."

"What'll get sore?"

"Guess."

"Oh."

"Uh-huh. You don't want to wear it out, do you?"

"Of course not."

"Then you better be careful," Margo told her, her eyes dancing. "You better be very careful. If it wore out you might have a hard time getting a new one."

It didn't wear out.

And, for two weeks, everything was quite perfect. For two weeks she and Curt were together almost constantly. They met after school and he drove her home then, if either of them had anything to do, he would leave her while she did what homework she had. They either went out for dinner or ate at her house, and then they did the thing they were doing so well together.

He wanted to stay the night—night after night he asked her if he could sleep all night with her, and each time she told him that she didn't want him to. After five or six nights like that he stopped asking.

The best thing about it, she thought, was that they were happy together even when they both had all their clothes on. It wasn't just a sexual relationship—they talked shop, listened to music, took in an occasional movie and spent hours at a clip just babbling about nothing at all. It was a full and rich relationship, and in that respect it was a very wonderful thing.

That wasn't the only thing. She could feel herself getting closer and closer to Curt, depending more and more upon him. Even if she never married him there was a very good chance that he would come to be a husband to her in fact if not in name. She didn't know whether she loved him or not, didn't know just what the word *Love* meant. But whether she did or not, she was coming closer to that four-letter state the more she went through a certain four-letter process.

And, if she went on that way, she wouldn't be true to Dana. Not by any stretch of the imagination. Not the way she was going.

It bothered her. There were times when she was sorely tempted to say to hell with Dana—not quite in those words, of course, but that was the gist of it. *Dana is dead*, she would tell herself at times like that. *Dana is dead and I loved him but he's gone now. Now I have Curt and he has me and that's all there is to it.*

But that wasn't all there was to it.

Love isn't a sometime thing, she would answer herself. *You can't love somebody and then turn it off and love somebody else instead. It just doesn't work that way. If you love a man you love him, period, and when he's dead you go on loving him and nobody else because that's the way love is and if you play around with it you're only going to wind up more confused than you already are, which is going some, even for you.*

So she was happy.

Marvelously happy.

Hysterically happy.

But confused . . . very confused.

The confusion reached the boiling point on Friday night. They'd been together almost two weeks—it would be two weeks Sunday—and that night he picked her up and took her out to dinner. They went to a Lebanese restaurant on Main Street where the shish kebab was served on a flaming skewer and where the atmosphere was almost as thick as the coffee.

Curved swords dangled from the ceiling. Weird Arabic music permeated the room and the odor of sandalwood incense was all over the place. They each had a couple of drinks before dinner and wine with the meal and she was a little unsteady on her feet when he asked her to dance.

The dance floor was small and cluttered with couples. They had to dance close together, which was fine with her, and they danced slowly because, logically enough, the music that the band was playing was slow music. Curt was far from being the best dancer in the western world, not to mention the Lebanese world, but he held her close and moved in time to the music and she enjoyed dancing with him.

He put his mouth to her ear.

He said: "I love you."

She didn't say anything but she trembled slightly. He had never told her that he loved her. And what bothered her more than anything else was the fact that she was glad to hear him say it.

"I love you, Barbara."

"Don't say that," she whispered.

"It's true."

"Don't—"

"I love you."

"Don't love me," she managed.

He held her tighter and didn't answer. The number ended and they left the dance floor. He paid the check and left a tip and they walked out of the restaurant.

In the car he kissed her and told her once again that he loved her, and when he went to kiss her a second time she stiffened and he let go of her. He sat and looked into her eyes for several seconds.

Then he said: "I think we'd better have a talk."

She nodded.

"Your place or mine?"

"I don't care."

"Let's try yours then."

He drove to her house and they didn't talk on the way. She sat close to him but not as close as usual and there was something between them, some sort of barrier that had not been there before.

He parked on the street in front of her house and they walked inside together.

They sat down on the couch.

"Barbara," he said, "things are a mess, aren't they?"

She swallowed.

"A mess," he repeated. "I love you, honey. You know that, don't you?"

"I guess so."

"I want to marry you, Barbara."

She couldn't talk—all she could do was shake her head from side to side.

"I want to marry you. I want you to marry me. We'd be good together, Barbara."

She didn't say anything.

"Why not?"

"I've already told you."

"Tell me something that makes sense for a change."

She didn't say anything.

"Don't you love me?"

"I don't know."

"Don't you want me with you all the time? When you wake up in the morning don't you sometimes wish I was there with you?"

"Of course, but—"

"But what?"

"But I don't want to marry you."

"Why not?"

"I told you!"

"All you've told me is a lot of nonsense! You tell me the same garbage every damned—"

"You don't have to shout at me."

He took a breath, sighed and let it out. "I'm sorry," he said. "I don't mean to lose my temper. You know that."

"I know."

"But I can't help it. I want you so much, Barbara, and I want to be everything to you. I want to be a husband to you, damn it."

Her eyes got a faraway look in them and she turned away from him. *I had a husband*, she thought. *One husband ought to be enough for a woman.*

"Don't you want to have children?"

Dreamily she said: "Dana and I couldn't have children. We wanted a child, you see, but the doctor told us we couldn't have one so we were going to adopt one. We had everything all set with the adoption agency but then—"

"Stop it."

"—he died," she finished lamely.

"Barbara—"

"He . . . died."

"Barbara, that's just it. He died—but you didn't. He was a great guy and you loved him but he's dead and buried and—"

"Not buried," she cut in, still speaking as if in a daze. "Not buried. He didn't want to be buried, you see, so he was cremated in accordance with his last wishes like it says in the newspaper stories and his ashes were scattered to the four winds, also in accordance with his last wishes. He had read about Thorstein Veblen, you see, and Thorstein Veblen had had his ashes placed in a stream that floated into the ocean. He thought about that, you see, and he thought about Joe Hill, how he had his ashes parceled out and passed out to people in little envelopes, but he decided he didn't want it to be that way, so—"

"Barbara!"

"—so he was cremated, you see, and he's not buried now even though he is dead, and—"

He slapped her. He slapped her hard across the face and she broke then. One minute she was staring off into space, her eyes wide and her mouth working and her brain in a trance. The next minute she was in his arms with her head on his chest and her tears flowing from her eyes and soaking into the front of his shirt.

"Barbara, honey, it'll be all right. Everything will be all right. Don't worry about it."

She went on crying. She couldn't stop.

"Let it go," he advised her. "I'm here and I'll hold you and everything will be all right. Just let it all go, honey. Everything will be all right."

Everything wasn't all right.

Everything wasn't all right at all.

Everything was terrible.

When she stopped crying finally they tried to talk things over sensibly and logically. But it didn't work, and they could see after awhile that nothing was going to work, that things were just going to keep on getting a little worse and a little harder to bear until they both quietly lost their minds.

It was a mess.

"Let's not talk about it any more," she said at last. "I can't take it, Curt. I just can't stand it."

He nodded, agreeing.

"Let's go upstairs," she said.

He looked at her.

She needed him now, needed him more than ever after what they had just gone through. "Come on," she said, catching at his hand. "Let's go upstairs, darling."

"No," he said.

"What?"

He disengaged his hand. "I'm not going upstairs with you," he told her. "Not now. Not tonight."

"What's wrong?"

He couldn't look at her.

"Curt—what's the matter?"

"I don't know. Nothing's the matter—but I don't feel like making love to you tonight. That's all."

"You don't feel like making love to me?"

"Not tonight."

"But—"

He turned on her, his eyes angry. "What the hell's wrong with you?" he demanded. "What in God's name is the matter with you?"

She didn't understand.

"You think all that matters is let's go upstairs and crawl into bed? You think everything can solve itself as long as the two of us are grinding our groins together? Is that what you think?"

"I didn't say that!"

"You don't have to." He lowered his eyes and when he spoke his voice was very flat, very level.

"Barbara, if you want somebody to warm your bed on cold nights you'd better find yourself another pigeon. I'm not the man you're looking for. Making love to you is a rare and wonderful treat but I'm not seventeen years old any more. I've been laid before, Barbara. I'm not an inexperienced kid with pimples on his face who doesn't care about anything but getting his rocks off. I'm too old for that."

He took a breath and continued. "Look," he said. "It's supposed to be the other way around—you're supposed to be the one who's holding out for the wedding ring, not me. But things are a little bit upside down and I don't like it."

"What do you want me to do?"

"You know the answer to that one."

She clenched her teeth and talked through them in an effort to keep her voice from breaking. "I'm not going to marry you," she said. "I've told you that again and again and again. What more do you want from me?"

Levelly he said: "I want you to shit or get off the pot."

When she stopped crying finally he took her by the shoulders and talked to her very softly. Every once in a while she would start to cry again and he would hold her closer until she got control of herself.

"Love isn't the starry nonsense you think it is," he kept saying. "A person can be in love more than once. For Christ's sake—suppose you never met Dana. Do you think you would have gone the rest of your life without falling in love with anybody?"

She couldn't answer that one. She didn't know the answer to it.

"I'm going," he announced at last. "I'm not going to make love to you, not until you've got some idea of what the hell you want. I'm not a stud horse, Barbara, and I'm not going to be used like one.

"And I can't compete with a dead man. When you're ready to count me in as a full partner, let me know. Until then you'll have to sleep alone."

She watched woodenly as he stalked out of the house and headed down the walk to his car. Then she stood staring out of the window as the car pulled away from the curb and headed on down the street. At the corner the car turned and disappeared from view.

Then she couldn't see anything—not even the street, not even the window an inch in front of her eyes.

Her tears were in the way.

She went to sleep more as a defense mechanism than anything else. She ran out of tears after awhile and couldn't cry any more— her only alternative to sleep was to lie awake and think about what had happened and that was out of the question. She couldn't bear to think about it, not now, not for the time being.

It would be better to sleep on it.

She got undressed and ready for bed. Then, when she was in bed with the covers pulled over her, she began to realize just how much she was in danger of losing, just how much she needed Curt.

If only he weren't so pigheaded.

Or, for that matter, if only *she* weren't so pigheaded.

Oh, it was his fault. The bastard—and he *was* a bastard, in addition to behaving like one—the bastard ought to be more understanding. If he just listened to what she was trying to say to him instead of letting his own notions get in the way—then things would be different. Then he wouldn't have stormed out of the house like a man possessed and she wouldn't be sleeping alone.

What was the matter with things the way they had been? He'd been enjoying himself and so had she. Their relationship was a nice, calm, warm sort of thing with no tension and no strings.

And now—

Now, for all practical purposes, their relationship had ceased to exist.

Which was a hell of a note.

She buried her head underneath the covers and tried to think. There had to be a way to work things out, a way to get Curt back without giving up her own principles. Besides, if she went back on her own principles, if she could force herself to change her vow, would that be any better? She's just being hypocritical about it all and Curt would be getting the smelly end of the stick whether he realized it or not. That was no fairer to him than the way things stood now.

I'm not a seventeen-year-old kid any more. He had said that, or something very similar to it. Was he right: was it childish to have a relationship without ties? Or was she right and was he being the childish one, the immature one, the one who demanded tangible proof of the importance of their relationship?

She couldn't think, couldn't get her mind to work right.

Whatever the answer was she decided that she would have a much better chance of figuring it out in the morning. Her mind would be clearer then and she would be able to look at everything through eyes that were able to focus properly instead of glaring at the world through the hole in the top of her head.

The morning would be better all around.

She pulled her head out from under the bedcovers and glanced at the alarm clock's radium dial. It was almost two—how had the time gone by so quickly? Well, it didn't matter. She could sleep as late as she wanted in the morning. It would be a nice lazy Saturday, a good time to get her mind straightened out and to figure out where she was going and what she would do when she got there.

She snuggled her head under the covers.

She closed her eyes.

Minutes later she was asleep.

She dreamed a very strange dream that night.

She dreamed that she was in a long dark tunnel, so long and so dark that she couldn't see any light in either direction. She was standing in the middle of the tunnel and she wanted to get out but she didn't know which way was the shorter, and for this reason she didn't walk in either direction. She simply stood there in the middle of the tunnel waiting for someone to come along and help her.

But no one came, and then off in the distance she heard a train whistle. The train was coming through the tunnel, and when she looked down she saw that she was standing in the middle of the railway tracks.

The train was coming closer. She saw that it was an old steam locomotive and that black puffs of smoke were coming out of the chimney.

If she didn't get out of the way the train would run her down.

But she couldn't move. She was in the precise middle of the tracks and she didn't know whether to jump to the right or to the left. She just couldn't make up her mind which way to leap.

And all the while the train kept getting closer, the puffs of thick black smoke became larger and thicker and blacker, the whistle was louder and louder in her ears and it became more and more imperative for her to jump.

But she couldn't jump.

Because she didn't know which way to go.

She screamed. She screamed for help, screamed for somebody to come and save her.

Nobody came. But off in the distance she could hear a voice calling to her, calling her name.

"Barbara," the voice called. "Barbara!"

It was Curt's voice.

"Jump!" he was shouting.

But she couldn't jump because she didn't know which way to jump. He was telling her to jump but she still didn't know which way to jump and all the while the train was coming closer and closer and closer.

•   •   •

She awoke with a start, realizing dimly that it was morning and that the dream was nothing but a dream. There was no train and no tunnel, and instead of the train whistle there was only the doorbell ringing. She slipped her bathrobe on and walked down the stairs barefoot, thinking that it might be Curt at the door, that he might be coming back to apologize, that then they could go back upstairs and he would make love to her and she wouldn't have any bad dreams from then on.

She got to the door.

She opened it.

It wasn't Curt.

Chapter 9

It was not Curt.

It was someone else entirely, someone whose name she did not know. She knew who it was, knew him very well as a matter of fact.

But she did not know his name. And, because she didn't know what else to do, she said the first thing that came to mind.

She said: "The furnace doesn't need fixing."

And the furnace repairman said: "I didn't come to fix the furnace."

Involuntarily she stepped back, clutching her robe tight around her. He shoved the door open and stepped into the house, closing it after him. She didn't know what to do. She wanted to scream but she didn't know exactly how to go about it.

"What do you want?"

He grinned.

"*What do you want?*"

"That's a pretty silly question," he said. "Strikes me that's a pretty silly question. I figure you ought to be able to guess what I want."

She shivered.

"No need to be all upset," he said. "It's not like I was doing something I never did before. Just because we won't be doing it bare-assed on the cellar floor is no reason for you to carry on so. You'll enjoy it just as much as last time, you can be sure of it."

"No," she said. "No, no you can't—"

He laughed. "Hell," he said, "I sure as hell can. Now look, Mrs. Sussex—it seems to me I did you a good turn a while back when you were ready to jump me you were so hard up. Now how about loosening up a little, huh?"

He reached for her and she backed away from him. He came closer and she tried to take another step away from him but the wall got in her way and all at once there was no place for her to go. His hands took hold of her shoulders and she shrank against the wall.

His breath was foul in her face. It was worse than the dream, worse than the long tunnel with the train coming and her feet stuck to the railroad track.

"No," she whispered. "No, please, no no no no . . ."

"Yes," he said, grinning down at her, mocking her. "Yes, yes yes yes yes."

He didn't kiss her exactly. It couldn't be described as a kiss, not when he took her poor face between his strong hands and hauled her up against him, kissing her so hard that he hurt her lips.

She struggled but his hands held her face tightly and she couldn't move. Then, when he kissed her a second time, when his mouth came down upon hers once again, she bit him.

She didn't even know what she was doing, didn't even realize just what was happening, but she managed to sink her teeth into his lower lip as hard as she possibly could, hard enough to draw blood, hard enough to make him yelp in a combination of pain and surprise and let go of her.

Then he did a strange thing. He burst out laughing and she couldn't even move from the spot where she was standing while he threw back his head and laughed so loud that the house shook with the force of his laughter.

"Awright," he said when he stopped laughing. "This'll make it more fun. You want to play rough, then we play rough. You're calling the shots this morning, Mrs. Sussex. We'll arrange the whole business whatever way you want it."

She didn't know what he meant. Not just then. Not until he hit her, and then she knew but then it was too late.

He hit her first in the face with his open hand and her head slammed back against the wall from the force of the blow. She saw stars and her brain reeled around crazily, but that was only the beginning.

Then he hit her with his fist, hit her in the stomach, sank his hard fist into her stomach so that she doubled up in horrible agony. Her robe fell open but she couldn't do anything about it; she was too busy clutching her stomach with both hands in an effort to ease the pain.

She couldn't even scream.

He took her by the shoulders then and he ripped the robe off of her and threw it across the room. She stood naked, shivering, her stomach one huge impossible pain and her head ringing. It was difficult for her to breathe and impossible for her to say a word or make a sound.

He hit her again in the same spot as before and she fell to her knees.

It was the worst pain she had ever experienced. The pain swelled in her breast until the whole breast seemed to have a pulse of its own; then the pain spread throughout her entire body. She collapsed on the floor, unable to function, totally and completely incapable of any action whatsoever, her whole soft body as limp as a wet mop.

She was just dimly aware that he was saying something, just dimly aware that he was taking off his own clothes and dropping them upon the floor. She was only slightly more aware of it when he lifted her in his arms like a fireman lifting a child and carried her up the flight of stairs to her room. He found the bedroom and shoved the door open; then he tossed her through the air and onto the bed. She landed face down and another jet of pain tore through her breasts where he had struck her.

"That was just the appetizer," he said. "Get set for the main course."

She wondered vaguely what he meant.

Then she found out.

Once, mercifully, she passed out.

She revived and felt an unbearable weight pressing down on her.

She passed out a second time, this time for good.

You go to sleep. Then, while you are sound asleep, someone prepares a fire and lets it burn down. You are still asleep and the someone who prepared the fire now takes you and heaves you onto the bed of burning coals.

You wake up.

And you feel exactly the way Barbara Sussex felt.

Her head ached with an ache that was worse than any hangover she had ever experienced, but that was the least of it. Her breast was all black-and-blue and spangled with burst blood vessels; it throbbed like an open wound. Her stomach was even worse.

She rolled over. It was equally painful lying on her back or on her stomach. She tried to stand up but she fell on her face almost immediately and it was with a great deal of difficulty that she managed to crawl back on top of the bed and bury her face in the pillow.

She remained in that position for over an hour. By that time the worst of the pain had subsided and she was able to walk to the bathroom and gulp down three aspirin and a glass of water. The aspirin helped—another hour later and she could think again, her mind able to grasp something other than the terrible pain.

She examined herself in a mirror. In a way she was lucky. Outside of a split lip her face was unmarked. And her body would heal, although it would take awhile before it looked as it had before he had come.

At one point she burst out into hysterical laughter. There was nothing funny about it but she couldn't control herself and she laughed on and on.

She had realized something which was suddenly very funny, very funny indeed.

She still didn't know his name.

•   •   •

Her fingers were shaking when she picked up the phone. She needed help. She wanted to call a doctor but the thought of a doctor seeing her the way she was and asking her how she had gotten that way frightened her. Instead she dialed Curt's number. He answered the phone after three rings and it made her feel better just to hear his voice on the other end of the line, just to hear him and know that he was there and she was not alone.

"Curt?"

"What is it, Barbara?"

"I . . . want to see you."

Silence.

Then: "Have you made up your mind, Barbara?"

"No," she said, "but I have to—"

"Barbara, I don't want to play silly kindergarten games any more. Maybe you don't realize that what the two of us went through last night is a fairly serious business."

"Please," she said. "Please come over—"

"I'm sorry," he said. "Not until you make up your mind, Barbara."

And he hung up.

At first she couldn't believe that he had hung up. She stood with the receiver pressed tight against her ear, saying *Curt, Curt, Curt* over and over until her voice broke. Then and only then did she replace the receiver and stare blankly ahead. She didn't know what to do.

She had to call somebody. For a moment she was at the point of dialing Curt's number again but she didn't even get the first digit dialed before shaking her head in disgust and slamming the receiver down. To hell with him! If he was going to be such a bastard with his all suffering holier-than-thou attitude, to hell with him!

She called Margo.

Margo picked up the phone right away and Barbara knew instantly that everything was going to be all right, that Margo was a woman and not a man and that Margo could never hang up on her as Curt had done.

"I need you," she said, simply.

"What's the matter?"

"I'll tell you when you get here, but for God's sake get over here fast."

Margo didn't say anything for a second or two. Then, quickly, she said: "I'll be right over. Hang onto your hat, honey."

The line went dead and she groped her way back to the living room to wait for Margo. Margo would be over as soon as she could—she wasn't like Curt, wasn't selfish and demanding the way he was.

Margo would help her.

She waited in a chair in the living room and she did not have long to wait. Margo evidently broke all existing speed records; it seemed just seconds after she had hung up the phone that the doorbell rang and she opened the door to let Margo in. Margo burst through the door with a snappy phrase on her lips but the snappy phrase died there unspoken the second she got a look at Barbara.

"Barbie! God above, what happened to you?"

"I—"

"Oh, God—don't try to explain yet. Let's get upstairs and see if we can't take care of you. Oh, God!"

Margo shut the door quickly and took hold of Barbara's arm, helping her to the stairway and up the stairs. It was hard walking but she leaned on Margo and let the smaller girl take some of her weight, and the two of them managed to get to the top of the stairs together.

Margo led her to the bedroom and made her lie down on the bed.

"Barbie," she said, "how in the world . . . no, never mind, you can give me the whole bloody story later. You're a mess, sweets. I'll see what I can do."

Margo disappeared, then came back with a jar of ointment from the bathroom. "This is supposed to be good for everything from broken bones to menstrual cramps," she said. "That's if you believe what it says on the label, which I don't. But it might help a little."

Barbara nodded without speaking.

"I gather you don't want me to call a doctor."

"No."

Margo tossed her head. "Which means some son of a bitch of a man did this. Was it Curt? If it was so help me I'll kill him no matter what you did to deserve it. Was he the one? Just tell me that."

"No," she managed. "It was somebody else."

"Well, thank God for that. Hold still."

She held still while Margo worked the ointment into her stomach. The bruise was all purplish there and Margo's fingers hurt her at first but she steeled herself to the pain and after a few seconds it didn't bother her. The ointment penetrated quickly and began soothing the area almost immediately.

"That helping any?"

"A little."

"Hold still, Barbie. God, if I ever get my hands on whoever did this I'll castrate the dirty son of a bitch. You poor kid, you poor little mess of a kid. Is this doing any good?"

"It feels a little better already."

And it did—the ointment combined with the soothing pressure of Margo's fingers was working wonders. Barbara could even begin to believe that she'd eventually feel better again, that sometime she would be able to move without pain shooting out from her stomach.

"God, what he did to your breast! He must have used a sledgehammer!"

"Just . . . just his fist."

"You poor thing. Let's see if the ointment helps any there."

The ointment helped. The combination of ointment plus massage helped tremendously and gradually the pain in her breast began to subside. Margo kept working on her, kept working the ointment into her pores, and she kept feeling better and better.

Finally Margo said: "Want to tell me about it?"

"Okay."

"If you don't want to—"

"No," she said. "I do want to—I have to tell somebody or I'll go crazy."

She told her the whole thing—from the time Dana died right up to the present. She told her about the first time with the furnace repairman when her desires had made her a more than willing partner in what happened between them, told her in full detail what had happened that morning when the furnaceman decided to pay a second call upon her. Margo listened from beginning to end without saying a word or revealing an emotion in her pretty face.

"God," she said when Barbara had finished.

"I'm ... all right, I guess. It could have been worse. He could have killed me."

"What that bastard did to you! Say, did you call anybody else before you called me?"

"Why?"

"I thought you might have given Curt a ring."

"I did," she admitted.

"How come he isn't over here?"

She told Margo what had happened when she phoned Curt. Margo's eyes went wide with shock. "You must be kidding," she said. "You mean to tell me that he didn't even wait to find out what was wrong?"

She nodded.

"That's just like a man," Margo said angrily. "They're the most self-centered sons of bitches in the world. He couldn't stop to think that there might be something wrong with you, could he? All he has to worry about is whether or not you're going to marry him."

"I know," she said. "But maybe it's better this way."

"How do you mean?"

"I might have married him," she explained. "I never wanted to but he might have managed to talk me into it the way things were going. Now there's no danger of that happening, not after all this."

"I should hope not."

"Margo, why was he like that?"

Margo shrugged. "Men are like that," she said. "All they care about is themselves. They're just after a woman for what they can get from her, whether it's sex or companionship or whatever it is."

"I suppose you're right."

"Of course I'm right. Otherwise he'd be interested enough in your welfare so that he'd take you on the terms that were best for you instead of trying to talk you into something you're not ready for."

She nodded, sleepily.

"Relax now," Margo told her. "Let me do some more ointmenting now."

She lay perfectly still while Margo worked the soothing cream into her belly and breast again. Margo's touch was lighter than ever, her fingers sure and gentle. She let her eyes close.

Margo's fingers continued touching her, stroking her. Barbara was half-asleep and half-awake, living in a world where her body floated in a blue-green sea with nothing in the world but Margo's sure fingers.

And Margo's mouth when it lowered to kiss her.

And Margo's voice, soft and gently husky, saying: "I love you, Barbie."

Chapter 10

Her eyes refused to focus. Her brain spun like a top, but all she could understand was that Margo was kissing her, Margo's lips were pressing hers, Margo's hands on her breasts were doing more than work the cream into her flesh.

Margo was kissing her.

Dimly she realized that she ought to be sick, disgusted, offended. The kisses of another woman ought to nauseate and revolt her.

But that was not the effect they were having.

She lay there, passive, submitting to Margo's caresses without batting an eyelash. And she had to admit to herself that she wasn't disgusted, not in the least. She rather enjoyed what Margo was doing to her.

She let her mouth open to admit Margo's insistent tongue and discovered that Margo was kissing her as well as a man might kiss her, even better than a man. And Margo's mouth was soft, so wonderfully soft. She never knew another mouth could be so soft, never realized that a kiss could taste so delicious.

She returned the kiss.

Margo kissed her again, her hands framing Barbara's face. Then Margo pecked a kiss on each closed eyelid and flicked her tongue at the tip of Barbara's nose. They kissed again and this time it was

Barbara who darted a warm tongue between two warm lips to taste and savor the sweetness of the other girl's lips and tongue. Almost without wishing it she was putting her arms around Margo's body, holding the small brunette close and returning her kiss with a superabundance of passion that she didn't have to fake.

The kiss was over. Now Margo was slipping away from her and she didn't want her to leave, didn't want Margo to leave her there all by herself. She reached upward and started to cry out, to tell Margo not to leave her, to stay with her and kiss her and touch her.

But Margo was a woman.

Well, so what? What good was a man? She'd had herself a man—two of them, since Dana died. And what good did they do her? One of them had beaten her so badly that she was lucky to be alive, and the other was so selfish and possessive and demanding that as far as he was concerned she could drop dead and he wouldn't care.

And, when she was beaten and sick and half dead, who had come to take care of her?

Not the guy who beat her up.

Not Curt, either.

Margo.

A woman.

So why shouldn't she want Margo to kiss her and make love to her?

No reason. No reason at all.

But Margo wasn't kissing her any more. Margo had left her, and now she was all alone on her bed with no clothes on. What in the world had happened to Margo? What in the world was she doing?

She opened one eye.

Ah. There was Margo. And that was what she was doing, the cunning little devil.

She was taking off her clothes.

Barbara watched fascinated as Margo stripped quickly and efficiently. Margo took off the suit jacket and the shirt, unbuttoned the plain white blouse and hung it on the back of a chair. Then she took off her bra and panties as casually as if she were getting ready for a bath and stood in the middle of the bedroom stark naked. Barbara had to catch her breath at the sight of her.

She hadn't realized before just how lovely Margo Kent really was. Margo had the type of body that looked much better naked than with clothes on. Her curves were soft and gentle curves, but when no clothing covered her milky white skin the curves were visible and exciting.

She couldn't stop staring at Margo's breasts. They were different from her own—much smaller, to begin with. But they were so perfectly formed, so firm and round and lovely, and the tiny nipples were such a deep shade of red!

What's wrong with me? I'm a woman. I'm not supposed to get excited by looking at another woman.

But she was getting excited; there was no way to deny it. And when Margo walked to the bed and sat down on the edge of it, her own pulse rate shot up and her heart was pounding a hole in her rib cage.

Then Margo stretched out on the bed. Less than an inch separated their two bodies.

The inch of air shrank.

It disappeared.

She wasn't sure what was happening, didn't want to think what was happening. She just wanted it to go on forever, wanted to spend her whole life with Margo in her arms and Margo's lips kissing her mouth and eyes and throat.

Barbara's passion mounted—but it was a new passion, a passion unlike anything she had ever known. She wasn't overpowered by it, wasn't urgent for a quick and desperate release from it. It was quite the opposite—a gentle passion that rose and rose to newer and greater heights, a passion equally uncontrollable but far more relaxed, far less demanding.

She put her hands on the back of Margo's neck and massaged the soft skin there, noting with pleasure that Margo was enjoying the caress. Then Margo wriggled a little on the bed and Barbara thought for a minute that it was because she wanted her to stop stroking her neck. But that wasn't it. Margo had found a new part of her to kiss.

Her breasts didn't hurt from the blows, not now.

Neither did her belly.

She didn't ache now, not any more, and it didn't seem possible that she had ever known any pain since the beginning of time.

Everything was too beautiful to have ever been spoiled by pain.

The world dipped and soared. The sky closed in on her and then retreated again. The earth and the sky merged, parted and merged again.

She opened her eyes and saw nothing.

She listened but heard nothing.

When it was finally over, finally finished, she knew what it felt like to be struck by lightning.

When it was over she slept. This was not strange—the beating alone had exhausted her, the beating and the emotional trauma that had accompanied it, and when this was combined with the experience of lovemaking the result, inevitably, was total exhaustion.

When she woke up she was not alone. Margo was there, holding her in her arms and looking down on her the way a mother looks at a sick child.

Before she could talk Margo opened her mouth to speak.

"Hi," she said, softly, gently. "Hi, Barbie."

"Hi."

"Sleep well?"

She nodded.

"Poor baby," Margo was saying. "Poor little baby. Are you feeling better now?"

"Lots better."

"Does it hurt?"

"Just a little."

"Poor little baby. Barbie—it was your first time, wasn't it?"

"Uh-huh."

Margo leaned over and kissed her on the forehead. "I knew it was," she said. "I was a grade-A bitch to take advantage of you but I just couldn't help it. You looked so damned lovely with those big beautiful breasts and that sexy mop of blonde hair. Can you forgive me, angel?"

"Forgive you? What's there to forgive?"

Margo smiled. "Dope—don't you realize what just happened? I made love to you, Barbie."

"I know."

"I . . . seduced you. Although you were so helpless that a purist might call it a case of rape. Aren't you furious with me?"

"No."

"You're not?"

"Why should I be?"

Margo chucked her under the chin. "Most girls would be mad," she said.

"I'm not *most girls*."

"I know."

"Besides," she added, "it wasn't rape or anything like it. I knew what you were doing. I could have stopped you if I had wanted to."

"You could have?"

She nodded.

"Then why didn't you?"

"Because I was enjoying it."

Margo got up from the bed and Barbara saw that she still hadn't dressed. The sight of Margo's body was having the same effect on her again. She let her eyes run up and down the slender white form from head to toe while Margo walked across the room to get a pack of cigarettes from her purse. When she came back with the cigarettes in one hand and a book of matches in the other Barbara went on staring and a smile appeared on Margo's face.

"Having fun?"

Barbara blushed.

"Don't be bashful, Barbie. I like it when you look at me like that."

Margo handed her one of the cigarettes and she put it between her lips. Then Margo scratched a match and lit both of the cigarettes.

"Barbie, do you have any idea what you're getting into? Or is all of this just happening while you sit around with wide eyes?"

She hesitated a minute before answering. "I'm not sure," she said finally. "Maybe you'd better tell me what's going on."

Margo smiled. "Okay," she said. "To start things off I guess you've realized that all the talk about men was nothing but camouflage."

"Haven't you ever—"

"Had a man? Once—and I didn't like it. I wasn't lying completely when I said I was busy getting banged when you called me and I wasn't home. I was getting banged, all right. Not by men. By women."

"Then you're a lesbian."

"What did you think you and I were just doing—picking forget-me-nots? I'm a lesbian."

"I thought . . . I guess I thought a lesbian was a woman with short hair and a deep voice and men's clothing and . . . and—"

"And hair on her chest," Margo finished for her. "Do I look as though I have hair on my chest, baby?"

Boldly she reached out a finger and touched the silky valley of skin between Margo's two perfect little breasts.

"No," she said solemnly. "Not a bit."

"I'm not the hairy-chested type. There are some lesbians like the type you just finished describing, Barbie—although I must say that damned few of them have hair on their chests. They're called butches—they dress like men, walk like men, talk like men, and do damned near everything but screw like men. I'm not one of them. Me—I'm a woman."

"I can see that."

Margo grinned appreciatively. "But," she said, "I am quite definitely gay."

"Gay?"

"Poor little thing—you don't know much of anything, do you? Gay means homosexual, which in this particular case means me. Get it?"

"Uh-huh."

"You get an A for brilliance," Margo said. "Now as a reward you may kiss me."

And she did.

"Margo," she said when the kiss ended, "how come you didn't try to have this happen before? Weren't you strongly attracted to me?"

"Like a moth to a flame, sweets."

"Then—"

"Then why didn't I have one hand up your skirt the second after we said hello the first time? Well, for one thing, it would have caused one hell of a lot of raised eyebrows in the cafeteria.

But that wasn't the main reason—I'm kind of used to raised eyebrows. Honey, I was scared stiff to make a pass at you!"

"Scared? Why on earth should you be scared of me?"

"For one thing, all you had to do was open your mouth and I would never have another job teaching as long as I lived. I had to be awfully careful. Then, when I knew you well enough so that I knew you wouldn't tell on me even if I did make a pass, I still was afraid. I put too much value on your friendship to risk losing it. See?"

"I see."

"Believe me," she went on earnestly, "I never thought this would happen, Barbie. I decided that you weren't gay and that you wouldn't want to go to bed with me and I figured we would just be friends. But I couldn't help myself."

"I'm glad it happened."

"Are you?"

"Of course. Margo, if all the men in the world are either like that guy who raped me or like Curt, I'm through with men. I've had a belly full of them."

"Then what do you want?"

Barbara smiled. She rolled over on her side away from Margo and stubbed out her cigarette in the ashtray on the night table.

Then she rolled back to face Margo.

"You," she said softly, her voice little more than a whisper. "I want you."

"Do you?"

"Yes."

"Are you sure?"

"I'm positive."

"Then what are you waiting for?"

"What do you mean?"

"Take me," Margo said, grinning. "I'm yours."

"But—"

"What's the matter, silly?"

"I don't know what to do exactly."

"You don't?"

"No."

"Remember what I did to you?"

"Of course."

"What the hell," Margo said. "You might try that for a starter. We can find other things to do later on, but you'll always get by just using your imagination."

They kissed, and now it was Barbara who was the aggressor. Margo's body seemed very small to her now, small and weak and defenseless.

And soft. Deliciously soft and smooth.

Gently she eased Margo back onto the bed with her black hair spread out on the white pillow. Then she leaned forward and kissed her on the mouth.

Margo closed her eyes and Barbara kissed her eyelids and her chin.

Then her throat.

Then the little hollow at the base of the throat where Margo's pulse was beating wildly.

Their lovemaking lasted for hours. When it was over they remained together, side by side, mouth to mouth, belly to belly and breast to breast.

And slept.

•   •   •

They were together all day Sunday. They woke up almost at the same time and at once they began to make love, and Barbara had almost forgotten what it was like to make love in the morning with her body half-drugged from sleep and her mind still not functioning, her whole being devoted solely to lovemaking. The transfer from sleep to wakefulness was made slowly, gently, with the medium of love far more effective than the combination of coffee and tobacco could ever hope to be.

Then she cooked breakfast for both of them and they ate together. After breakfast Margo had to get back to her apartment and Barbara was grateful for the opportunity to be alone. She had a lot to think about.

"You come to my place for dinner," Margo said. "I want to cook for you."

"What'll you cook?"

"Nothing too difficult—I'm a pretty lousy cook. But come over anyhow."

After Margo had gone she got dressed and went out dutifully to pick up her copy of the Sunday *Times*. After all, there were certain parts of her routine which couldn't be disturbed. She gave the *Times* a very quick reading and then sat down with a record on the hi-fi and a cigarette in her hand to think things over.

She had never thought of herself as a lesbian and she still didn't. Lesbian—the word itself—seemed to imply that the person so named was the member of some grand and glorious sorority with chapters throughout the world. And she just didn't feel like a sorority sister.

But at the same time she definitely felt like a woman who would be more than content to spend the rest of her life sleeping with another woman.

Which, by all the rules of the game, made her a lesbian. A four-star gold-plated lesbian.

She closed her eyes to concentrate. She knew very little about lesbianism, about abnormality, about herself, for that matter. But she did know a few things and they seemed to be enough for the time being.

Number One—she would be perfectly happy if she never saw a man as long as she lived. Curt, for all she cared, could go to hell for himself. He could jump off the Peace Bridge with a bowling ball soldered to his neck.

Number Two—sleeping with Margo Kent had turned out to be a tremendously pleasurable experience. One which would be repeated.

Did that make her a lesbian? She didn't know and didn't care. What she did know was that she was going to continue sleeping with Margo and that she was never—repeat: never—going to spend another minute in bed with Curtis Tyrone.

That was elementary.

And, strangely, she didn't feel guilty or disgusted or any of the things a person was supposed to feel.

Not at all.

In fact, all things considered, she felt better than she had in months.

•   •   •

She had dinner at Margo's apartment that night. Margo got around the cooking problem by broiling a pair of thick steaks, and if she was a lousy cook the steaks didn't show it. They were delicious.

They ate by candlelight, which Barbara discovered could be even more romantic when it was two girls who were doing it than when the diners were she and Curt. After dinner she helped Margo with the dishes; then, when they were washed and dried and put away, they returned to the living room.

The candles were still burning. Margo put a record on the hi-fi—she was a relatively rabid jazz fan—and they sat down on the couch.

And took off each other's clothes.

Slowly.

And made love.

Very slowly.

And sat up talking on into the night and made love until they were properly (or improperly, dependent upon how you looked at it) exhausted, and fell asleep in Margo's single bed with just enough room for the two of them.

And woke up in the morning. And had breakfast together in the little breakfast nook.

And went to school together like two very prim and proper schoolmarms.

She saw Curt in school that day. Strangely enough she hadn't dreaded seeing him again, had hardly thought about it in fact, and when he took her arm and led her aside after classes were over for the day she followed him dutifully and looked at him vacantly, wondering how she could have cared at all about him. Why, he had even expected her to marry him! It seemed ridiculous now, but that was what had happened.

"Well?"

"Well what?"

He forced a smile. "I've gone crazy without you," he said. "But I've been trying to give you enough time to come to some sort of a decision. Have you?"

She looked puzzled.

"Well, have you?"

"Have I what?"

"Have you come to a decision?"

Her mind wasn't on what he was saying; the whole conversation seemed very unreal to her.

He asked her again.

"What kind of a decision?"

"About you and me."

"About us?"

"Yes," he said, patiently. "About us."

You man, you, she thought. *You big stupid rotten lousy man.*

And she said: "Yes. I've come to a decision."

"Well?"

She was seeing him for the first time—the red hair, the broad shoulders, the rugged face that might have been chiseled from stone.

Levelly she said: "I'd just as soon never see you again for the rest of my life."

He was stunned. He started to say something but she didn't stay around to see what it was. She walked down the steps and out of the schoolyard without a backward glance, walking quickly away from him.

Away from him.

To somebody else.

To Margo.

Chapter 11

The next week was a period of adjustment. Barbara and Margo lived together—they were with each other almost all of the time, either at Barbara's house on Covington Road or at Margo's Delaware Avenue apartment. Barbara's education in the methods and manners of lesbian love was brought to a high level of accomplishment. Practice, in this area as in any other, seemed to be making perfect.

At the same time she found herself learning a tremendous amount about the twisted subculture of lesbianism, the gay world. First Margo told her as much as she could; then she gave her a book to read. The name of the book was *Strange Are The Ways Of Love*. It was a novel by someone named Lesley Evans and it told her some of the things that Margo hadn't been able to get across to her.

Curt tried once more to get in touch with her but she made it clear to him that she couldn't be less interested in seeing him. She was more than happy without him, happy to spend her days in school and her nights with Margo. That was more than enough for her.

She and Margo rarely went out together. For one thing, there weren't too many places they could go unless they were careful to conceal their relationship. While two women could dine together or go to a movie without arousing suspicion, there was more than a little likelihood that passers-by would turn around to stare at a short brunette and a tall blonde who held hands and necked in public. And when she and Margo were together they found it terribly difficult to keep their hands to themselves. Margo was always touching her, kissing her, taking her arm. And she was acting in much the same way toward Margo.

Besides, they had enough to do just getting used to each other. It was a joy to spend a quiet evening either at her house or at the other girl's apartment, talking and reading and listening to music and making love. Gradually she was teaching Margo to like classical music while Margo was busy making a jazz fan out of her. They didn't have to go out—they had enough fun just being together.

But Saturday night they went out. They had dinner at Barbara's house that night and Margo made her announcement over coffee.

"Dress up nice tonight," she said. "We're invited to a party."

"A party?"

"Some friends of mine," Margo explained. "All girls."

"You mean—"

"I mean they're gay, natch. A nice crowd, too—I think you'll like them. Only you'd better not like them too much, kitten."

Barbara found herself grinning.

"I think you'll enjoy yourself, Barbie. You haven't had any contact with a gay crowd yet since you crossed over the bridge. We'll just drop over for a few drinks so you can get an idea of the sort of people we are."

Barbara nodded. Actually the idea wasn't too attractive to her.

She was curious, naturally, and she couldn't help wanting to see what the other gay girls were like—what they looked like, how they acted, what they talked about and what they did at their parties.

But at the same time she was a little reluctant to go, although she didn't show her reluctance to Margo. She didn't think of herself as a lesbian but as Margo's lover, and there was an important distinction. By going to the party she would be proclaiming herself as one of the gay set, as a lesbian. By living with Margo she retained her identity as an individual without committing herself to any group.

"Honey?"

She looked up.

"You don't seem too enthusiastic."

"I am," she said. "I really am."

"Sure—you're a ball of fire."

"I—"

"Look," Margo said, "you're probably feeling a little jealous and I can understand that. Naturally I've had affairs with some of the girls you'll meet tonight. But that's all over and done with—I've got you now, kitten. So don't even think about it."

She nodded. That was a side to it that she hadn't even considered until Margo mentioned it. And that part, strangely enough, didn't bother her at all.

"What'll I wear?"

"Something sexy," Margo advised. "I want everybody to see what a nice fish I caught. Why don't you wear that jersey thing of yours?"

The blue jersey thing fit like a glove except that it didn't make what it contained look like a hand. On the contrary—the blue jersey thing was worn without benefit of bra or girdle and looked rather like woad—the blue dye that the ancient Britons had painted on their nude bodies to terrify the Roman invaders. It was, all things considered, quite a spectacular outfit.

They took Margo's car to the party, which was at Lucy Roscommon's home on Middlesex Drive. The house was a huge brick-and-stone affair with ivy growing up its walls, and Margo told her on the way over that the home was part of the settlement Lucy got from her ex-husband.

"She tried to go straight," Margo explained, "but the way it turned out she wound up with a faggot who was also trying to go straight, and the two of them together just managed to make each other miserable. Finally he was sleeping with another guy and she was back with an old girlfriend of hers, so they decided to take the mess to Reno. He gave her the house and some fabulous alimony—they're still friends, as I understand it. Only they don't see too much of each other."

Barbara shook her head wonderingly. There would certainly be a unique bunch of girls at the affair and she wasn't sure how she would handle herself.

Margo pulled the car to a stop in front of the house, turned off the motor and pulled up the emergency brake. She got out on her side of the car and winked briefly to Barbara, who was still sitting in the car. Bravely Barbara opened her door and got out.

"Chin up," Margo was saying. "Don't be so damned scared of your own shadow. I think you'll wind up enjoying yourself tonight."

She smiled quickly and they started for the door. Margo took her arm as they walked and Barbara started to draw it away, then realized that where they were going everybody would know about their relationship the instant they walked in the door.

A huge brass doorknob was located in the exact center of the massive oak door. A mother-of-pearl button in the middle of the knob served as a doorbell.

Margo rang it once, then once more.

The door swung open.

Everybody seemed to be having fun.

That was her first impression as she looked at the bevy of pretty girls scattered throughout the room. Her second thought was that they didn't look like lesbians at all. Then she thought that she didn't look like a lesbian herself, and that neither did Margo, and that therefore that whole line of thought was a waste of time.

Then somebody was pushing a drink into her hand and she smiled gratefully at the little redhead who had handed it to her. The drink was properly cold and properly alcoholic and she took a long sip of it.

"I'm Lucy Roscommon," the redhead announced. "And you're Barbara—is that right?"

"That's right."

"I've heard a good deal about you, Barbara."

Lucy's last remark had her wondering for a moment and she was at the point of asking the girl just what she had heard when Lucy vanished into the other room, distributing more drinks to some of the other girls and reclaiming empty glasses. Instead she managed to latch onto Margo and the two of them found seats on a couch in the living room.

Margo clapped her hands, shouting *Introduction Time* at the top of her lungs, and the conversation in the room dropped to a dull roar. Quickly she went around the room, introducing each of the girls present to Barbara.

Then, after the introductions had been made and forgotten, she told Barbara a little about each of the girls.

"The gal with a pixie haircut is Sandra Shore," she whispered, "known as Sandy Shore for short. She's a Gal Friday for a lawyer downtown and the poor dope's been trying to make her for years. He doesn't stand the chance of a snowball in hell, poor guy. Sandy practically dies if a man comes within ten feet of her. She's real paranoid about men.

"The blonde in the corner who could stand to lose ten pounds or so is Pamela Kerry. She's an awfully sweet kid but she's terribly promiscuous. Why, I know for a fact that she's slept with every girl in this room."

Including you, she thought but didn't say.

"Including me," Margo said, winking. "But don't forget—that was before I met you. You can't hold it against me."

Barbara found herself grinning. "Anyway," she said, "Pam hasn't slept with *every* girl in the room. I'm in the room, and she hasn't had me."

"Stay away from her," Margo said a bit sternly. Then her face relaxed. "The willowy brunette on the chair is Andrea Cumberland. She's in interior decorating. You know, they say every interior decorator in creation is a fairy. They forgot about Andrea when they figured that out—she's quite the opposite, wouldn't you say?"

Barbara nodded.

"Andrea and Sandy used to go together," Margo went on. "Then Sandy left her for Lucy—you couldn't blame her, really. Andrea's business was in pretty sad shape and Lucy had enough money to keep Sandy very well. But Andrea's still pretty blue over the whole thing. I'm surprised she showed up here. She and Lucy weren't speaking for awhile."

"Does everybody switch from one person to another all the time?"

"Well, not everybody and not all the time. But it's pretty much like that, Barbie. The gay life is a regular round robin, a hands-around sort of thing all the time. It's hellish."

Without thinking she said: "And what about us? Will you just get up and leave me one of these days? Is that what's going to happen—you'll find somebody else and then I'll find somebody else and—"

"Barbie!"

"Well, I can't help—"

Margo stood up. "This is too public," she said. "Come on in the kitchen. I want to talk to you."

Barbara stood up and Margo took her by the arm and led her into a large kitchen. She closed the door, shutting out most of the noise of the party. Only occasional laughter floated through the door now.

"Listen," she said, "I don't want you to talk like that, Barbie. You poor idiot—I love you. I'm not going to run out on you. I'm only scared that you'll run out on me."

"I'm sorry, Margo."

"I shouldn't have brought you here," Margo said. "We had it nice enough just staying by ourselves. We should have stayed home tonight."

Barbara didn't say anything.

"Do you have a cigarette?"

Barbara took two cigarettes from her purse, gave one to Margo and lit them both. Margo took a long drag on hers and blew smoke at the ceiling. Then she forced a smile.

"Give me a kiss," she said.

They kissed. Margo kissed her hard, passionately and almost desperately. She clung to Barbara as if the kiss could dispel the barrier that seemed to be creeping up between the two of them.

It couldn't.

Because, throughout the kiss, Barbara couldn't help thinking that something was wrong. She returned Margo's kiss with equal passion in order to drive the thought from her head but it persisted.

I shouldn't be here, she thought. *I don't belong here. This isn't for me.*

"Barbie—"

She shook her head in an effort to clear it. "Come on," she said, valiantly. "We'd better join the party again or they'll think we're doing something positively immoral in here."

And, without wanting to, she thought that what they were doing was positively immoral.

The thought was galling.

Back in the living room again the party was in full swing. She took a drink and gulped it down gratefully, feeling the alcohol beginning to take hold of her. Margo drifted off to talk to somebody else and she was left alone to watch the party, to talk to the girls and to watch them talking to each other. When Lucy Roscommon came up to talk with her she felt a little bit lost, a little bit unsure of herself and uncomfortable with the short redhead.

Lucy was cruising her, she thought. Lucy Roscommon was sizing her up and hinting that she would like to have Barbara for a lover. And, automatically, Barbara began to wonder what it would be like to sleep with Lucy.

It might be interesting, she thought. Lucy was an extremely pretty girl. She was short, very short—about the same height as Margo. But their proportions were radically different. While Margo was very slender and petite, Lucy seemed to be all breasts and buttocks. Barbara had never seen such large full breasts on such a small woman.

To take those big breasts in her hands, to kiss the tips of them, to hold Lucy Roscommon in her arms and do all the exciting things to her that she could—

God, what was she thinking of? What in the world was the matter with her?

She managed to get away from Lucy, managed to get off in a corner by herself. Her mind was all mixed up and she wanted a little time to herself.

Time to think.

The thoughts that came to her were painful ones.

Disturbing ones.

To begin with, she began to see the roomful of lovely lesbians in a new light. *Gay* was a ridiculous term to apply to them; they were anything but gay. They were miserable, most of them, flitting from one bed to another, living in constant fear of discovery and exposure.

Was this the kind of life she wanted for herself? More important, was this where she belonged?

It wasn't.

She remembered with a start the way her life had been before Dana died. Her relationship with Dana had been full, full and complete. It was the sort of thing she hadn't even come close to achieving with Margo.

She was just fooling herself. She wasn't cut out for the gay life, not Barbara Sussex, not her. She liked Margo and she would always like her, but she couldn't go on living with her. It just wasn't right for her. She didn't know what she needed, but Margo couldn't offer it to her, whatever it might turn out to be.

That much she knew.

She spent a long time sitting and thinking, sitting and watching the other girls. She couldn't feel any sense of kinship with them no matter how she tried, and she came to realize that this was due to the fact that no kinship existed. She wasn't a lesbian.

She could turn into one. If she kept on going with Margo it wouldn't be long before she was a full-fledged member of the group. Pretty soon someone like Lucy Roscommon would cruise her and would turn out to be just too appealing to resist. Then she would break with Margo and start living with someone else— and then she'd be on the merry-go-round, going from girl to girl, spending her time at gay parties or in gay bars.

That could happen—if she let it happen.

But she wasn't going to let it happen.

She stood up suddenly, walked across the room to where Margo was talking with another girl and tugged at Margo's arm. Margo turned around, a little annoyed at the interruption, but something in Barbara's eyes kept her from revealing her annoyance.

"Let's go, Margo."

"What do you mean?"

"Let's leave. I don't want to stay here any more."

Margo started to protest but she caught something in Barbara's voice and didn't say anything. She nodded quickly and the two of them went to say goodbye to their hostess.

Lucy Roscommon held Barbara's hand an instant too long when they were leaving. She smiled and there was more in her smile than friendship.

"Come and see me," she breathed. It was an open invitation and nothing else.

"That bitch!" Margo said when they were in the car. "She has to cruise at her own goddamned party. Is that why you wanted to leave?"

"No. That's not it."

Margo turned the key in the ignition, started the car. "It isn't?"

Barbara shook her head.

"Then what's the matter?"

Barbara hesitated. She took a deep breath and let it out slowly. She fumbled for a cigarette and her fingers were trembling when she tried to strike the match. Finally she managed to get it lit.

"What's wrong, honey?"

"I'm ... not ... gay," she managed.

"Huh?"

"I . . . don't belong here, Margo. I just don't fit in. I'm not a lesbian."

"You're not?"

"I don't think so."

"What the hell have we been doing for the past week—playing mumbledy peg?"

"I—"

Margo sighed. "We'd better have a talk," she said. "And it's not the sort of talk we ought to have in a moving car. We might just wind up wrapped around a telephone pole. Hold everything until we get to your place, huh?"

They held everything.

They got to Barbara's place.

Inside, on the couch, Margo said: "Okay—let's get going. What gives?"

"I already told you."

"So? You want out?"

"What do you mean?"

"You want us to quit sleeping together?"

"I don't know."

"Well, what the hell do you want?"

She couldn't answer. She lit another cigarette and offered Margo one but the brunette shook her head.

"Let's get this thrashed out, Barbie. You want me to tell you what you want? I don't want to, but I guess it's about time."

She was puzzled.

"You want a man," Margo told her. "You've wanted a man all along. That's all you ever wanted."

"What!"

"Yes," Margo said. "Listen to me now because I know what I'm talking about. You've wanted a man all along—you wanted Curt Tyrone, as a matter of fact, and you wanted to marry the guy. But all this crap inside your head about remaining true to your husband kept you from accepting Curt's proposal. You wouldn't even live with the poor son of a bitch—because you sensed that he was man enough to take Dana's place.

"But there was never any worry of me taking Dana's place and as a result you didn't mind having me spend the night with you. Now you've finally managed to figure out that the gay life is not for you. I suppose that's part of the reason I dragged you along to that shitty party—so that you could see what you were getting into. I could have hung onto you for awhile yet if I wanted to, but what the hell. I like you too much, Barbie. This isn't the life for you and you've got a chance for a life that's a good deal better. I don't want to stand in your way."

Barbara swallowed.

"You want Curt," Margo told her. "He was a little dense— that's why he handed you such a hard time. But don't forget the kind of a time you gave him with this off-again on-again business. Meet him halfway, sugar. Everything'll work out for the two of you."

"I don't know what to say."

"Say? What's there to say? Hell, there's no problem, kitten. We've had fun, haven't we?"

She nodded.

"So what's the problem? You'll wind up with Curt and I'll latch onto somebody else for the time being. I think I'll go back to the party and give Lucy hell for the way she was making a heavy play for you."

She giggled. "On second thought," she said, "I think I'll give her hell first and then see if I can't get in her pants. She's a good-looking bitch, that Lucy. And she had the hots for me not too long ago. It shouldn't be too hard to edge Andrea out, at least for tonight."

Barbara smiled. "Good luck," she said.

"Thanks."

"Find out if that red hair of hers is her own or if it came out of a bottle."

"I'll let you know." Margo stood up. "Why don't you give me a kiss goodbye, Barbie?"

It started out as a sisterly sort of kiss; then Margo's grip on her shoulders tightened convulsively and the shorter girl caught her breath.

"Barbie," she gasped. "Just once more, kitten. Just once more for old time's sake. Please?"

"All right."

They walked hand-in-hand up the staircase to the bedroom. There they undressed quickly, methodically, and Barbara drew back the bedcovers and they stretched out together on top of the bedsheet.

They kissed.

They touched each other.

They began to make love.

Margo was no longer what she needed, and she found herself faking the responses, feigning the passion that she did not feel any more.

Then it was over, and involuntarily Barbara felt herself withdrawing to her own side of the bed, moving away from Margo.

Margo laughed.

It wasn't a happy laugh.

"See? You don't want me any more. I'd better go now, honey."

Barbara couldn't answer.

"We can still be . . . friends," Margo went on. "I'll never stop liking you, honey."

"I . . . I'll go on liking you, too."

"Good. Will you invite me to your wedding?"

Barbara smiled. Her wedding—she would be having a wedding now, if Curt would have her, if he still wanted her. She would have to find out.

And she said: "Of course, Margo. You can be my virginal bridesmaid."

Chapter 12

Margo was gone.

That much was obvious, and stating that much alone didn't tell her anything. Now suppose she carried it one step further:

Margo was gone.

She was left.

Still incomplete. There ought to be a formula that would fit everything in, all the stray pieces of the jumbled jigsaw puzzle, all the oddments and endments. Surely there was a formula somewhere. Perhaps if she were a math teacher instead of an English teacher the elusive formula would reveal itself to her.

Margo was gone.

She was left.

Curt was available.

Now that was more like it, except for the nagging fact that it took one point for granted. The last point wasn't provable from the known facts. The last point, when you stopped to give it some serious thought, was something of a ticklish subject, an eternal unknown.

There were, you see, several questions.

Did she want Curt? Now that was one hell of a puzzler. Sober reflection brought her to the realization that the new-found knowledge that she didn't want to spend her remaining days on earth bedding down with other girls did not perforce mean that she wanted Curt to slip a ring onto her finger. Her arguments against marriage still carried as much weight as ever, didn't they?

Well, didn't they?

Perhaps they didn't. The whole episode with Margo had dredged up a lot of miscellaneous trauma, and if nothing else she was beginning to realize that her whole notion of remaining true to her husband's memory was a good deal less valid than it had seemed to her. If it was the sort of notion which led her alternately to rape and lesbianism, there might well be something haywire somewhere.

She dressed quickly, walked downstairs and got a cigarette started. It tasted foul and she stubbed it out after a puff or two. Then, after she sat around for a few more slow-moving minutes and chewed on her nails for exercise, she lit another cigarette. This one didn't taste as bad as the other.

She did a lot of thinking. It was difficult to dope everything out—analyzing yourself is rarely simple stuff. But she lit the cigarette at 10 o'clock, finished it a few minutes later, and by 10:30 she had some of the answers. Not all of them, but enough so that she could see where she had gone wrong—and why.

She had loved Dana. He was her first love, her great love, a man as important to her as her own life.

Okay.

Then he died.

And, for this reason, her little mind had made rules of its own, simple little rules that went like so:

If you love someone, he'll die.

And you'll be alone.

And hurt.

Therefore, if you love someone you'll be hurt.

Ergo—don't love anybody.

She had been afraid to love, lived in fear of it. But her mind had to invent a more rational reason for her own refusal to love. That's where being-true-to-Dana had come into the picture.

But it didn't make any sense to "be true to Dana"—not when you looked at it that way. Dana himself would have been the last person to ask it of her; in fact, he had been careful to urge her quite explicitly to find someone else after he was gone.

Afraid to love. That was why she had been more willing to accept the embraces of the repairman than those of Curt. That was why she would accept a woman like Margo as a love partner—because the love they shared wasn't true love, and the break-up they went through was a relatively painless affair.

But now she wasn't afraid any more. Now she was afraid *not* to love, afraid of the twin possibilities of a life by herself or a life as a lesbian. She didn't want either of these lives, not now, not now that she had her eyes open for once.

She wanted a man.

A husband.

A man who would love her and be loved by her.

A man, in short, who was a bastard in the original sense of the word but not in the figurative sense of the word. A man with a big chest and muscles in his arms and flaming red hair.

A man named Curt Tyrone.

•   •   •

There was, she thought slowly, only one problem. It was entirely possible that Curt didn't want her any more, that he didn't give a damn whether he ever saw her again. He had loved her—that much she knew. But after the way she treated him it wouldn't be surprising if he couldn't stand the sight of her now. And where would she be then?

If that were the case, she thought, she would not be in very good shape at all.

She stood up, brushed ashes off her skirt and headed for the telephone. There was one surefire method of finding out how Curt felt about her and all it demanded of her was a total loss of pride. Well, to hell with pride—there were more important things at stake than pride.

She dialed Curt's number. She didn't have to look it up. She hadn't forgotten it.

He answered midway through the third ring. "Hello?"

"Hello," she said. "This is Barbara."

He didn't say anything and she wondered what was going through his mind. Would he hang up on her?

"I wanted to talk to you," she said. "I . . . I have to see you. It's important."

"What do you want?"

"Can't I tell you as soon as I get over there? It'll just take me a few minutes to drive over. I want very much to see you, Curt."

There was a moment of silence. Then he was saying: "You don't give a fellow much of a break, Barbara. I'd just about managed to get you off my mind for five or ten minutes at a time and now you want to see me. I . . . I don't know whether or not I ought to let you come over."

"Curt—"

He didn't let her get started.

"I suppose I can't live with you," he said, "but that doesn't do a hell of a lot to change the fact that I can't very well live without you, either. Hang on—I'll be over as soon as I can."

"I can drive to your place if you'd prefer."

"No," he said, "stay where you are. I ought to have my head examined, but I'll be right over."

She waited for him to hang up, then returned the phone to its cradle and stood for several seconds staring at it without seeing it. The first part of the battle was won—he still cared enough about her to want to see her. But he was afraid, too. Very much afraid, afraid she would hurt him again. That was why he had hung up on her when she called him after she had been beaten by the repairman—and if she had used her head she would have been able to realize it then and there.

But he still loved her, and now that she was ready for him this was very important. She loved him now, and she had never told him that she loved him.

Well, she would tell him now.

She walked into the bathroom, washed her face and made it up again. She had put the blue jersey dress on again and it still hugged her body perfectly, which was just as well. There was no harm in using sex as a weapon. She needed every weapon she could get her hands on.

She turned out the bathroom light and closed the door after her when she returned to the living room to wait for him. She didn't have to wait long. She was hardly seated on the couch when the bell rang, and instantly she sprang to her feet and headed for the door.

A handful of glib opening lines were on the tip of her tongue when she threw open the door. They died there unspoken when she saw him, died and were forgotten as she flung herself into his arms.

His arms tightened around her. He held her and she felt alive again, newborn and young and alive, and she wanted him to hold her forever.

She said the only thing she could say.

She said: "Don't let go."

They were sitting on the couch drinking screwdrivers because she didn't think she would be able to talk until she had a drink working inside of her. The two strong drinks she had had earlier in the evening had worn off long ago and she needed a lift in order to say what she had to say. She finished the screwdriver in three large gulps and turned to face him, her nerves unsteady and her fingers trembling slightly.

She said: "I love you."

That was all she could say, all she could think of, all that was important to her. It was the first and only time she had told him and she saw the way his face seemed to melt at the news, the way he took a deep breath and smiled slowly and gratefully.

She said it again.

He didn't say anything; it wasn't necessary. He took her in

his arms and kissed her and the glass dropped from his hand and spilled what was left of his screwdriver on the floor.

It made a mess on the rug. She didn't give a damn about the rug.

When he kissed her the second time everything was all right and she knew that everything would always be all right, that there was nothing to worry about from now on, that they would be married and have children and be happy, happy forever, and that nothing would ever come between them again. It was hard to believe now, now when he was kissing her and loving her, that she had ever refused to marry him.

But she had. And something definitely had to be done about that.

She let him kiss her a third time. Then she pushed away from him and got up from the couch. He looked at her, asking her with his eyes what was the matter, and she told him with her own eyes that nothing was the matter, nothing at all, that nothing would ever be the matter, that everything was absolutely fine and would be absolutely fine until the end of time.

She stood before him, a smile playing with the corners of her lips.

Then she got down on her knees.

He still didn't understand and she wanted to laugh out loud. But she didn't laugh. It wasn't time to laugh now. It was serious— deadly serious, and she had to approach the problem with the proper attitude.

She folded her hands like a penitent, like a worshipper at a heavenly throne, and in a very small soft meek voice she said: "Curtis Tyrone, will you marry me?"

She had her eyes closed while she proposed and she didn't open them so she couldn't see the expression on his face. He didn't say anything at first and by that time she was afraid to open her eyes, even afraid to listen because she was worried that he would refuse her.

Then he said: "Try and stop me."

She opened her eyes and discovered that they were moist with tears. Then he had his hands under her shoulders and he was lifting her, lifting her high in the air and setting her on her feet. He hugged her close and her heart almost stopped beating. She took a quick breath, then let it surge from her lungs like air from a blown-out tire as she collapsed against him, her knees unable to support her weight any longer.

He was stroking her hair. "Everything's all right now," he told her. "We had a rough time there for a week but now everything's all right. And everything's going to stay all right."

He led her to the couch and helped her sit down; then he sat down beside her. After a few deep breaths she was all right again—now she felt all giddy and lightheaded and what she said didn't make an enormous amount of sense but she said it anyway.

"We'll have a gigantic, enormous family," she said. "We'll have six beautiful girls with long blonde hair and we'll name them all Hector."

"Hector?"

"Definitely," she said. "What else can you name six girls with long blonde hair?"

"If you put it that way I guess it makes sense."

"And six boys with gorgeous bright red hair," she went on, undaunted. "Six at the least."

"What'll we name them?"

"Hector," she said. "What else?"

"The boys and the girls will all be named Hector?"

She nodded.

He thought about it for a minute. "What the hell," he said, "I'll bite. Why?"

She pouted. "Can't you guess?"

"Nope."

"It's simple," she said. "When you call *Hector* they'll all come. You can send away the ones you don't want."

"Oh."

"Now do you understand?"

"Couldn't we just name them all Cora instead?"

"Don't be ridiculous," she said. "You couldn't name them all Cora. It would be foolish."

Then they both started laughing. He laughed the way a man ought to laugh, giving it everything he had. They went on laughing for a long time, letting go of everything that had been bottled up for so long, letting their emotions dissipate in laughter.

"Curt? What did you do all week?"

He shrugged. "Nothing much."

"Nothing at all?"

"Not really. Thought about you most of the time. That's about all."

"But you didn't call me."

"I couldn't," he said. "I had to let you come to me. That's the only way it could work out."

"Did you just sit around the apartment?"

He shrugged again. "I got drunk once," he said. "Went out and found a prostitute."

"How . . . was it?"

"Mechanical," he said. "Lousy. I picked up a slut on Allen Street and traded five dollars for a quick experiment in mutual boredom. Not much fun at all, I'm afraid."

"Was she pretty?"

He grinned. "I honestly don't remember what she looked like. I didn't even notice."

"Was she as pretty as I am?"

The grin spread. "If she had been," he said, "I'd have been sure to notice."

"You're sweet."

"So are you."

"And you're going to be my husband."

"Right."

He kissed her again.

"Barbara?"

"What is it, honey?"

"What did you do all week?"

She thought about what she had done all week, thought about the repairman who raped her and Margo who slept with her, thought about the things the two of them had done. And all the events of that week seemed as though they had happened centuries ago. The details were already beginning to blur in her mind.

Some day she would tell him. Someday, perhaps, he would learn about Margo.

But not now.

"Nothing much," she said. "Nothing important."

Huskily he said: "Let's do something important, Barbara."

"Do you think we should?"

"I don't see why not."

"I don't know," she mused. "I'm not sure I know you well enough."

He didn't say anything. Instead he put his hand under her dress and did something to her to show her that she damn well *did* know him well enough. She squeezed her thighs together to hold his hand in place.

"Besides," she said, "maybe we ought to wait until we're married."

"Sure."

"We should," she said, trying to keep a straight face. "It's immoral."

"The hell it is."

"Well, isn't it?"

"It's bad enough you need a driving license and a hunting license and a fishing license in this goddamned state," he said. "I'll be damned a thousand times over before I'll concede the need for a sleeping license."

"You're real romantic."

"Romantic? I'm sex starved."

She pursed her lips, then squirmed a little when he wiggled his fingers. "Sex starved?"

"Yep."

"Honestly?"

"Yep."

"What the hell," she said with abandon. "Let's have a meal."

•   •   •

It was the most wonderful thing that had ever happened to her in her entire life. It was as if they were a pair of eager virgins tasting the flavors of sexual love for the very first time, and it had all the delicious ritualistic trappings of such an experience.

He turned off the overhead light and left a light burning in the closet. It cast a shallow glow over the room that was just right.

He undressed her very slowly then, taking off her clothing, rolling her stockings down over her thighs and knees and calves. She stood perfectly still while he undressed her completely.

Then he made her turn and face the wall while he removed his own clothes. All the while he didn't touch her any more than he had to. Then, when he was nude too, he walked up to her from the rear and began to touch her, slowly, gently, languorously. She tried to take it calmly but it was quite impossible and when she couldn't stand it any more she whirled around and fell into his arms.

Then they were on the bed, wrapped up in their love for each other, moving together, loving, tasting and drinking deeply of each other.

The wedding was small, private and quick. Neither of them wanted a church wedding, both of them figuring that, as Curt put it, "God had better ways to waste his time than to oversee another damned wedding." They were married by a Justice of the Peace in a small town a few miles east of the city line.

A friend of Curt's, an army buddy named John Siencewicz, was the best man.

Margo Kent was bridesmaid.

No honeymoon—a wedding night in Buffalo's best hotel for a change of scene, but no time to take a trip. They both had to teach and couldn't get the time off. But it didn't make any difference, Barbara decided. Just being together—that would be enough of a honeymoon.

It might be tough sledding, she thought. They both had a lot of adjusting to do, a lot of learning about each other to get under their belts. But they loved and needed each other and that would get them off to a good start.

They'd make it.

It would work.

Even, she thought, even if they didn't wind up with six golden-haired girls and six carrot-topped boys. All of them named Hector.

My Newsletter: I get out an email newsletter at unpredictable intervals, but rarely more often than every other week. I'll be happy to add you to the distribution list. A blank email to lawbloc@gmail.com with "newsletter" in the subject line will get you on the list, and a click of the "Unsubscribe" link will get you off it, should you ultimately decide you're happier without it.

Lawrence Block has been writing award-winning mystery and suspense fiction for half a century. You can read his thoughts about crime fiction and crime writers in *The Crime of Our Lives*, where this MWA Grand Master tells it straight. His most recent novels are *The Girl With the Deep Blue Eyes*; *The Burglar Who Counted the Spoons*, featuring Bernie Rhodenbarr; *Hit Me*, featuring Keller; and *A Drop of the Hard Stuff*, featuring Matthew Scudder, played by Liam Neeson in the film *A Walk Among the Tombstones*. Several of his other books have been filmed, although not terribly well. He's well known for his books for writers, including the classic *Telling Lies for Fun & Profit*, and *The Liar's Bible*. In addition to prose works, he has written episodic television (*Tilt!*) and the Wong Kar-wai film, *My Blueberry Nights*. He is a modest and humble fellow, although you would never guess as much from this biographical note.

Email: lawbloc@gmail.com
Twitter: @LawrenceBlock
Facebook: lawrence.block
Website: lawrenceblock.com

www.ingramcontent.com/pod-product-compliance
Lightning Source LLC
Chambersburg PA
CBHW070551180626
46817CB00005B/1786